The Lost Ode

By

Virginia Slachman

2014

Cooper Dorian Books

St. Louis, Missouri

ISBN-13: **978-0692255292**
ISBN-10: **069225529X**

First Cooper Dorian Books edition July 2014

For information about special discounts on bulk purchases, please contact Cooper Dorian Books at cooperdorianbooks@gmail.com

Manufactured in the United States of America

Cover design by: redhotcreativesauce@yahoo.com
Cover photo credit: Maria Antonowitsch and Renaissance Rescue Ranch.

For Lauren

Acknowledgements

I'd like to thank several people whose generosity made this project possible. First, my thanks to Barry Irwin, founding partner of Team Valor. Without his assistance, I would not have met Steve Johnson, co-owner and managing partner of Margaux Farm, the thoroughbred breeding farm in Midway, Kentucky, where I lived for a time doing research for the book. Without both Barry and Steve's help, this book would not exist.

As well, thanks to my long-time friend Jim McCown for his scrupulous editing help, the entire Margaux Farm crew for allowing me to tag along for vet checks, feedings, and so on. And again, I thank Steve Johnson for setting up my interviews with veterinarians and visits to other area breeding farms, all of which figured directly into the creation of this book. Everyone I met in Kentucky during my research treated me with cordial generosity.

And finally, I'd like to thank Barbara and Laurence Hutchinson for the wonderful work they do at Renaissance Rescue, giving a new start to thoroughbreds coming off the track. Working there has taught me much about the intelligence, heart, and grace of these wonderful animals.

The Lost Ode

1

I'll be frank; I'm much more comfortable in the library doing research than I am most anywhere else. Much better in climate-controlled reading rooms than engaging in "small talk" at social events. When I'm not teaching, I work in the "Horschow Library of Antiquities and Classical Literature," a staid, gray-granite building with stone lions guarding the doors. Eight hours with my nose in a book is my idea of the perfect job.

Which is why doing this particular sort of favor for my colleague and IT whiz, Gwyneth, was high testament to our friendship. Left to my own devices, the Fasig-Tipton horse sale is the last place you'd find me. Yet there I was. Gwyneth's boyfriend was two people shy of a catering crew, so at the last minute we were recruited.

On the other hand, I was killing two birds with one stone. Gray Burke, owner of a Kentucky thoroughbred breeding farm, had asked my boss at the Horschow to authenticate a painting purported to be by John J. Audubon. Since both of us would be at the horse sale, I had agreed to pick up the painting.

To pass the time after refilling the buffet, I'd wandered into the auction room. One after another, the glistening bodies of very large horses stood for sale in the spotlight just below the auctioneer's stand. The yearlings were well-muscled and majestic. It took all of about thirty seconds for one to be bid into the high six figures by a man in the balcony who did little but raise an index finger.

I then wandered out to one of the rings, a covered one since the day had warmed, and watched the horses parade in and around and out. The Miss America pageant has nothing on the Fasig-Tipton horse sale, and I was told this is the "little sale," the real money being spent at Keeneland by sheiks and Europeans who jet in for the September yearling sale. I glanced around. Lots of young men and some women—most of them wearing khakis and some shade of blue shirt—leaned on the rails studying the horses, jotting notes now and then on pads. Everyone was on the lookout for the next superhorse. I'd heard Mine That Bird went for $9,500 here and won the Kentucky Derby. So it happens. That's what seemed to be on everyone's mind. It happens, why not to me?

A tap on my shoulder, and I was reminded of the reason for my visit. One of the reasons. I glanced at my watch, calculating how much time I'd been absent from buffet duty.

"Gray Burke," he said, extending his hand. "You're Julia?" When I nodded, he smiled and glanced behind me to the horses. "I was told to be on the look-out for someone in a white apron with blond hair," he said. "Thanks for making the trip." He tipped his head toward the ring, gesturing toward the horses. "Your first sale?"

I told him I knew next to nothing about horses.

He stepped beside me, and I turned to watch with him at the rail. He looked to be around 30, had dark brown hair, and the requisite uniform: khakis and a blue oxford cloth shirt with rolled up sleeves. He pointed his folded paper at one of the horses just making its round on the far side. "That's one of mine. He's out of Colton, and I'm

8

hoping he'll do well for us." He studied me a moment. "Gosh, sorry," he said, "you're here for the painting, not the horses."

I supposed, in his world, everyone at the sale had one frame of reference: horses and money, either coming in or going out.

Gray then explained that he'd put the painting on his desk in the office, gotten sidetracked, and come to the sale without it. "I completely understand if you don't want to take me up on this, but my farm's not far and if you'll come back with me, I'll put the painting in your hands and drive you back home myself." He looked sincerely apologetic.

"Sure," I said, thinking why not? "I'd enjoy seeing the farm." As an academic, my normal activity was to have my head in one book or another; I'd never been across the Ohio River, so a visit to a breeding farm in Bluegrass Country seemed intriguing. We made plans to meet up after Gray's horse went up in the next round. The buffet was about to shut down, so one more round of freshening its contents and my catering duties would come to an end.

After the Colton yearling sold, and not for the money Gray had hoped, we hopped in his black Navigator and took off for parts unknown, but as we were in Lexington, Gray's farm wasn't far.

Remnants of winter sped by outside the frosted windows; dirty snow mounded on the shoulder, bare oak and maple limbs stood stark beside evergreens lining the highway. The fact that I so quickly missed the cozy confines of the classics library reflected my serious distaste for cold weather.

As we drove, Gray explained that Brookfield Stud had been in his family for generations; begun in Virginia, Gray's great-grandfather had moved it to Lexington a few decades after the Civil War. Gray had been raised on the farm, learned to ride and handle breeding stock on the farm, and seldom left it. Except, he said, for his stint at Harvard. His father had passed away some time ago; he'd inherited Brookfield and, since his mother's retirement, ran the enterprise himself.

Gray soon turned off the highway onto a smaller, two-lane road with a browned grass divider—Paris Pike—and we traveled past the Lexington Country Club, Gainesway Farm, and one gated drive after another lined by un-mortared stone or black, long-railed, four-slat fencing. On either side stretched fields, with barns and houses set well back from the road. It was a Robert Frost sort of landscape, I thought. Not Andrew Wyeth, not stark and vacant, but filled with quiet life and, though I didn't know it at the time, death, too.

As he talked, I realized that other than the anomaly of his college education, his world did seem confined to a hand-span circumference on the map he had me get out of the glove compartment.

"See there," he pointed as I opened it, glancing from the road to the map, "there's Claiborne Farm, Calumet is there, Three Chimneys, Gainesway, which we just passed. All the major breeding farms are right under your nose."

"So Louisville and Lexington, that's it?" I asked. It seemed odd that the thoroughbred world would be confined to two cities in one state.

Gray put his wrist on the wheel and leaned back in his seat.

"Not really," he said. "Not any more. There's the Irish, the South Africans, the sheiks. And in the sixties and seventies, we sent a lot of runners to Europe. And of course England."

"Well," Gray said, after a time, as he sat up in his seat and peered to the right, "here we go."

10

Up ahead stood two stone pillars with square lanterns atop and a small plaque that read "Brookfield Stud" and, below that, "since 1876." Then we turned up the long, tree-lined drive ending in a gravel parking lot adjacent to the dark wood and limestone office. Gray parked, jumped out, and ran around to open my door. He offered a gloved hand, and I took it.

The stud farm, or what I could see of it, stretched out in rolling, black-fenced hills in all directions.

"How about a tour?" said Gray. "Then I'll get the painting into your hands." He smiled. "Promise."

I was intrigued. Gray's family had been breeding racehorses for over a hundred and thirty years. That's a lot of history. "Sure, " I said, but then was interrupted.

Gray's two-way went off at his belt.

"Go ahead," he said into the static.

The line crackled and I heard a woman say, "John's busy, can you come to Barn One? I have a sick foal I need someone to look at."

Gray smiled apologetically, said he'd be right there, then we got back into the Navigator, made a left over the stream, and parked in the gravel lot in front of Barn One.

"John's breeding Raj. Sorry," said Celia as we strode into the barn. A soft, maternal nicker sounded in a quietness otherwise marked by an occasional stamping or shuffling through bedding. John was the farm manager who, I learned, Celia would normally call for something like this.

"He doesn't have a fever," she told us as we approached the sick foal's stall, "but he's in a sweat and panting, and he just doesn't look good to me."

We looked in as Celia mentioned the drugs she'd administered: ulcer meds, an alcohol bath, meds for bacterial infection, and meds to open his bronchial tubes. "I waited about thirty minutes, but he's not nursing."

She peered in beside us.

"And now he's down."

In the stall the bay mare stood drowsing to the left. On the straw lay the foal, the little brush of his mane standing straight up and the small sweep of tail limp along his tiny, rounded hindquarters.

"He's tenting," said Celia, commenting on his state of dehydration.

Gray didn't need to see more. "Call Tim," he said. Then, "The others go down this quickly?"

"Yes," she said.

Gray frowned.

Celia glanced at the foal. "But not *like* this."

Gray said to me. "We've lost more than our share so far this year."

"Too many," said Celia.

I didn't say anything.

"Tim will take a look, send him to the hospital if he needs it."

Under her breath, Celia said, "Lot of good that's done. "

"Let me know," said Gray. He took my arm and guided me out of the barn into the bright light of day.

As we drove from the barn toward Gray's office, I was quiet. I was curious about Celia's comments, but I was there for the painting and, evidently, a tour, not to butt into Gray's business. Still, seeing that small foal in the stall made me wonder about the others they'd lost. He'd seemed so vulnerable and helpless. I supposed that was the other side of what had appeared such a glamorous business at the horse sale a short time ago.

A thin cover of snow still lay on the ground as we drove, dotted by the tips of new grass shoots, yet the white stillness was fresh against the dark black fences except where the horses had strayed. Gray gestured to the left, up

12

the rise. "Over there is the foaling barn and the mares barn, the lay-up barn, and then over there is the yearling barn." He glanced at me now and then to gauge my response. It was a calming scene, one that made me breathe easier; white low-slung buildings scattered over the rise and to the left and right. I could picture it in late spring, the mares being led down the gentle slope, crossing the bridge under which the clear stream flowed, then on across the grass, onto the gravel, and into one of paddocks or pastures. The slow slopes into the distance seemed peacefully maternal and suggested a deceptively simple life; a rural, cyclical existence in which life and death were held in equitable balance.

The appearance was deceptive. I wanted more information about the foals, but I sensed Gray didn't feel like talking about it. I reined myself in, so to speak, and then smiled. Language, I thought, will be the death of me.

Little did I realize how close to the truth that would be.

2

We arrived at the office building and stood for a moment on the parking lot looking toward the north. "Those are the stallion barns," Gray said, pointing just off to the right behind the office. He pointed beyond the small barns. "Back of that is the breeding shed."

Though we hadn't been standing very long out on the gravel drive, the cold had made a home inside my parka. I hugged myself and shivered; finally Gray noticed.

"Let's get you inside," he said. "Didn't mean to freeze you to death."

A tall, reedy fellow in blue jeans a few sizes too big had walked over from the first stallion barn and followed us in. He wore a yellowish parka, which in fact was olive green but had been splashed so often by inept bleaching or stallion meds, it appeared an off-shade of yellow. His straw hair matched the splotches. He had a run-down, tired look to him that made me think he was much older than the twenty-five or so he likely was.

He went right to the coffee pot in the reception area and poured himself a large Styrofoam cup.

Gray introduced me to him as Brett, one of the stallion grooms, later confiding that his early ambition had been to become a jockey but a spurt of growth had precluded that. Now he cared for the stallions he had once hoped to ride.

Brett simply nodded at the introduction, capped his coffee, and left.

Gray's office was spacious, with a big window that looked out onto the stallion barns over the neat hedge right outside the window. The stark light coming in made the dark paneling shine as if waxed, and on the wall opposite his big rosewood desk were pictures of horses crowded above the wainscoting: conformation shots, photo finishes, races caught in the backstretch, mares with foals rendered in relatively new and very old photos. Though there were a few grays and blacks, most of the horses were bays or chestnuts. Between the pictures hung bridles with gleaming bits and a crop or two. Here was history in its most tangible form. I wandered the wall, moving from faded old black-and-white photos to more recent ones in gleaming color.

The room smelled of leather and oil, and I turned to see Gray looking at something on the computer. Behind his desk hung etchings and faded, blurry pictures dating back to the days on the Virginia farm and, of course, interspersed with those were more horse photos.

Gray sat back in his chair and motioned for me to sit. He seemed to have put the foals out of thought. For the moment. He swiveled and starting pecking at the computer, calling up the stallions.

"Here, let me show you the heart of the farm." I moved beside him to see the screen. "The boys are booked well for the season," Gray said, turning to me. I saw a list of names scroll by: Serious Chances, Ataway Raj, Medes, Aurora's Prospect, Schism, Circuit Breaker, Antienne . . . names that bespoke a pedigree and hope more to do with market recognition, often, than racing ability, or so said Gray. These stallions had bowed tendons bad enough, won

15

enough, been hit in the joint with enough cortisone to warrant a stall for the few years it took to see if they could stamp themselves on their offspring and so live out life between the stall, paddock, and breeding shed . . . or, if not, be provided a permanent exit visa to Canada, Venezuela, or South Africa. And in the event they couldn't make it abroad, some suffered a fate worse than exile.

Gray motioned toward Medes' shining, muscular form on the screen, telling me to stay away from him. "He's a nightmare," said Gray. Then seeing my question before I asked it, he continued, "It's his feet. Makes him crazy. We have to hand-walk him, no turnout."

Gray turned back to the computer, clicking on a video of Medes moving. He walked with grace, I thought, every gleaming muscle.

"Any other horse with laminitis that bad, we'd put him down," said Gray. But he stressed Medes bred well, though mercilessly, rearing on his sculpted hind end and walking, roaring, into the often trembling mare, twitched and rigid at the breeding wall. Gray pointed to the screen. "His yearlings sell in the six figures." He turned to me, stating the obvious—"He earns a lot"— then shrugged.

"We couldn't manage it all without help," said Gray. He mentioned his long-time investor, Horace Laroveneur, who had a major stake in Medes. In fact, Gray said, Horace's family had been associated with Gray's for two generations, and the breeder had a financial interest in numerous other stallions standing at Brookfield, most notably Gray's two most promising newcomers—Aurora's Prospect and Schism. The Laroveneurs boarded their mares at the farm and bred to the stallions, which made a sort of incestuous economic sense.

It had worked for two generations and, as Gray quoted Horace, "If it ain't broke, don't fix it."

Gray ended with a comment about Medes. "I'll

show you when we get out to the barn—he's nearly kicked the bars out on his stall. That would be the cast iron bars," said Gray.

I nodded, making a note. Don't go into Medes' stall. I would remember that.

Gray stretched up and clicked out of the website. "How'd you like to see these guys in person?" I nodded and Gray shrugged on his parka and held mine out for me.

"Then let's get some coffee and see the boys."

We headed over to the stallion complex, Gray taking my arm, explaining how important "the boys" were to the bottom line. The thoroughbred business, he said, had shifted from the track to the breeding shed, making Brookfield's financial health the product of a fickle equation balancing mares in foal, to foals on the ground, to yearlings in training, to two-and three-year olds racing, to stallion stud fees, to mares booked, to mares in foal . . . and the cycle began again at the first of the year, year in year out for the past several generations.

We headed through the hedged yard at the side of his office. There were graves there, about ten along a row by the far hedge and then another five or so set at a right angle to them. The older headstones were crumbling and the names were etched, but blurry.

"Is this a cemetery?" I asked. Though the sun shone, I felt suddenly chilled.

Gray paused on the walkway, dropped my arm, and held his coffee out to the one in the corner. "Yes, that's the oldest one, Beau Lyons. He traces tail-male back to a great speed sire from England who stood at Virginia for my great-grandfather."

I walked over to the headstone. It was chipped and crumbly, leaning into the snow.

"There's his hooves, and heart, and head down there," said Gray. "That's what makes a great racehorse.

17

That's how they buried them in the old days." He took up my arm and steered me onto the walkway. Not looking at me, he said, "Some say his balls are there, too, but I can't say for sure."

We crossed to the stallion barn, where he slid back the door, and I looked in at two stalls to the right; their doors were whitewashed wood about chest high, then there were black, scrolling wrought iron bars the rest of the way up. It was quiet in there, though I did hear a regular shoosh, shoosh, shoosh of bedding to the left, on the far side of the barn.

On the stall doors hung shiny brass memorial plaques bearing the names of famous former inhabitants. I walked to the nearest one and read "King's Pen."

"He was a great horse, by Princequillo."

Gray mentioned the accomplishments of horses listed on plaques affixed to stalls at our right and left. They went back generations. It was an impressive heritage—Derby and Preakness winners, and many horses who'd earned well over six figures.

We stopped in front of a stall with three brass plates. "This is Aury's stall."

I bent my head toward the bars. The stallion lay in the straw, a huge shadowed chestnut curve of muscle, his back to me, his neck arched, his head drooping.

"He's sleeping," Gray said, and sighed. "This is one of the guys I'm really counting on . . . Him and Schism—they're my future." There was an intensity to his words. Gray's hand hung on the bar as he peered into the stall. "We really need a break-out stallion . . . That's all we need, one good year."

I wasn't sure who Gray was talking to at that point. It didn't appear to be me. He seemed worried, so I took it as my cue to ask about the foals Celia had referred to.

Gray hesitated but then seemed relieved to talk

18

about it. He didn't know me; I supposed, with not much at stake, it was a chance to vent.

Gray said he'd lost a number of foals in the last three months, but the numbers weren't enough to warrant alerting Rood and Riddle, the renowned equine hospital—Brookfield was still within "normal" foal losses at around ten percent. However, he said, the farm was used to doing better than normal—much better, in fact, and he seemed really concerned.

January and February are light foaling months, but now in late March, as the season got underway in earnest, the worrisome deaths occurred either in utero or on the ground fairly soon after birth, just as in 2001 when the Mare Reproductive Loss Syndrome hit Kentucky and thirty percent of the thoroughbred crop had died. A small enterprise relative to the larger breeding farms in the area, Brookfield's present financial state was precarious; the generations-long tradition Gray felt bound to continue was threatened. The foal deaths were potentially devastating.

But it wasn't MRLS this year, Gray said. Surrounding farms didn't have unusually high foal deaths. His tone turned serious.

"I'm not oblivious to foul play," he said, the furrow between his eyes deepening. "I know this can be a bad business." Then he was quiet for a time. He frowned and shook his head. "I just don't know what to think."

He didn't seem moved to continue, so we walked on. I felt his uneasiness, though, as if the foal deaths—even in low numbers—signaled something was wrong.

We stopped a few stalls down the way where Serious Chances plodded steadily around the interior perimeter, his head and muscled neck bobbing rhythmically. His human counterpart of like mentality would be wearing headphones.

The air shot straight out of Chance's oval nostrils in

an opaque steam. He was getting himself heated up a bit.

"Danced every dance," said Gray.

And still at it, I thought.

Suddenly Gray's two-way went off again. A man's voice came through: "Breeding barn, Gray. Now!"

I could hear the words clear and the urgency behind them. The alarm in Gray's eyes was immediate. He raced out the way we'd come, me trailing speedily behind. The man's face had paled, and he broke into a run, sprinting the distance between barns, then halted.

A trim man had stepped past the sliding barn door and held up his hand, his face anguished.

Gray halted. "Shit," he said. "Don't tell me, John. Not Schism."

The farm manager's stricken face glanced from me to Gray. "Heart attack seems like."

Gray visibly slumped, his hands on his hips, head bowed to the gravel. "God damnit," he whispered.

"He's gone," said John. "Breeding fine, then . . . "

Gray glanced up.

"There wasn't anything any of us could do," said John, "he was gone before he hit the ground."

3

I'd assured Gray there was no need for him to take me back over the river himself, in view of the circumstances. He seemed more sorrowful than angry, and I got the impression that the loss of one of his two best stallion prospects brought him more grief than concern for the bottom line.

"I'm really sorry, Julia," he'd said, escorting me to the truck. He'd asked Juan to drive me back to Cincinnati, and I stood to say goodbye holding the rolled up painting he'd given me, feeling at a loss as to what to say.

"Hold on," Gray said and sprinted back to his office. He returned in a few minutes with a brown parcel. "Here," he said holding it out as he opened the door for me, "I nearly forgot this. This journal goes with the painting. There's entries in it that show the painting is really Audubon's. I haven't read it all the way through, but anyway, they both go together." He looked stricken.

I gave him an awkward hug. He looked like he needed it. "I'll call you to follow up on the painting," he said, "when things calm down around here."

I hoped they would.

I had an hour drive to think about events at the

farm. Juan didn't speak much English, and we both seemed ok without attempting small talk. Which, of course, I'm no good at anyway.

I don't know, maybe when you're right in the middle of things, events don't seem as ominous or, as they did to me in this case, as intentional as they really are. I wondered at Gray's acceptance of so many bad things happening to his horses. I'd been there all of three hours, and one horse had died and a baby seemed close to it. Plus there were the deaths of the other foals he'd mentioned. I don't know, call me suspicious, I had a feeling that something was not right.

The truth was, I liked Gray. He seemed like a good man carrying the weight of a very large family heritage squarely on his very broad shoulders. At the moment, it seemed, that heritage was in jeopardy.

I had a momentary urge to tell Juan to turn that F150 right around and speed back down to the farm. I wondered if things were actually as wrong as they'd seemed or if it was just me, harboring suspicions where no suspicions were due.

Let's just say that appearances actually can be deceiving, or as in this case, deadly.

Once home, I jogged up the stairs to my apartment, painting in one hand, brown-wrapped parcel in the other. I retrieved my extra set of keys and trotted back down to the car Gwyneth had politely dropped off on her way home, and set out down the road to the doggie day care to pick up my big white pooch, Albert. Big, as in 130 pounds, and the male love of my life. He's so white he gets lost in the snow, but winter is definitely his time of year, and it does my heart good to see him lope across the distances. Living in the city, I have to drive quite a ways to let him off leash for a run. Most of the time it's long walks in the park, which is also good. He's handsome and a good boy, and I couldn't wait to have his slobbery hello kisses.

Once back home, I changed my clothes, fed Albert, and we both settled into our routine. I live in three huge rooms, plus galley kitchen and large bath, in a turn-of-the-century gray stone Victorian house that I own by way of converting it into three apartments—one to each floor. I live in the middle since I don't have need for the huge kitchen and conservatory on the first floor (I kill plants and don't cook) or the tiny rooms and five-flight walk-up from the basement of the third floor. I like my home with its fourteen-foot ceilings, ten-foot high windows, original parquet hardwood floors, Rookwood fireplace mantles, and the three-minute walk to Eden Park. I like not taking care of anyone but Albert, not having to ask about dinners out or how much I spend on doggie toys and treats. It's not the safest neighborhood in the city, but it is one of the prettiest.

After the news I made a fire, and with Albert's white mound at the foot of the couch, I took my half-full, cut-glass goblet of sherry and settled down to unwrap the parcel Gray had given me. Given the work I do, I went straight for the journal. The rolled painting stood in the corner.

It was a diary of sorts; its dated entries spanned the year 1841. I thumbed through the book, glancing at pages here and there and finding those towards the end most anxious-sounding due to the impending death of the writer. At the beginning of the book, on the front page, was the inscription: "George Keats," and below that was this: "a book of days in my own hand."

That was weird. Why authenticate your own diary?

There were also several loose sheets of very old paper shoved into the diary. I carefully lifted them out and set them aside. They seemed written in a different hand from the journal and were brittle with age. I lifted the top one to read:

The evening before yesterday we had a piano forte hop at Dilkes—There was very little amusement in the room . . .—Some people you must have observed have a most unpleasant effect upon you when you see them speaking in profile.

Indeed, I thought.

I returned the sheet and selected another dated the same month and year: January of 1820. There was a large slur of ink, then a small legible section:

I was surprised to hear of the state of Saciety at Louisville, it seems you are just as ridiculous there as we are here . . . Give my compliments to Mrs. Audubon and tell her I cannot think her husband either good looking or honest— Tell Mr. Audubon he's a fool.

I lay the journal on my lap. The date 1820, the reference to Louisville, the name "George" coupled with "Audubon" piqued my interest. As a scholar of British literature, from these few journal snippets, I had an inkling of what I had. This last entry had suggested it. I turned back to earlier-dated sheets to verify my hunch. I found this, dated 18 December, 1818:

I feel I must again begin with my poetry— for if I do not write, I am in pain—and obliged to smother my Spirit and look like an idiot at these requisite frivolities . . . I think you knew before you left England that my next subject would be 'the fall of Hyperion."

I put the journal down, sympathizing across the

centuries with feeling like an idiot at parties. But it was the last sentence that intrigued me.

"The Fall of Hyperion" is a poem by John Keats. I had done some research on Keats just last spring and learned that John's brother George had immigrated to America with his 16-year old bride Georgiana, settling in Louisville, Kentucky. This George had befriended the "Mr. Audubon" referred to in the letter much before Audubon became the celebrated naturalist he would be in future years; in fact, at the time of John's letter, Audubon (George felt) had swindled him. I supposed this is why Audubon is referred to as a "fool." The sheets I held in my hand appeared to be original letters written by John Keats to his brother, George.

This would be astounding, if what I held was genuine.

I sipped my sherry. I added a log to the fire and glanced out the window to the light snow falling in the twilight.

As Gray had said, there was the reference to Audubon. I'd have to read through everything closely to see if the painting Gray had given me was mentioned. The whole thing would take some sorting through; the loose papers were letters written in a different hand than was the journal, and I was sure they were penned by John.

Needless to say, I was up very late reading. What I found was more than intriguing. Though the entries might authenticate the painting, the journal also contained clues to what might be an even bigger find.

As the night wore on, I became increasingly excited by what I learned.

When I need a sense of order, I normally take notes, so sometime after two in the morning I nudged Albert out of the way and shuffled over to my desk where I retrieved my yellow-lined pad of paper and fine-point pen. After lobbing another log on the fire, I wrote down information about the two most pertinent issues.

First, it was clear that George and Georgiana *had* lived with Audubon—there were a lot of entries about how, during their earliest days in America, they'd been taken in by Audubon and his wife Lucy. As I've noted, this was much before Audubon became Mr. John J. Audubon, ornithologist and painter of great repute. In his early days, Audubon was a great hulk of a man fond of wearing leatherskins as he stuffed and wired reeking dead birds into paintable poses. To the great consternation, evidently, of his wife as well as George and his young bride. Perhaps Gray's painting was among those rare, early Audubon paintings. We'd have to wait for the Horschow to work its magic.

Secondly, and to me more exciting than the painting or the Audubon/Keats connection, was something incidental, something I could never have anticipated finding.

In the entries relating to George as his famous brother's critic and copyist and in what I felt were John Keats' letters to his brother, were indications that George had an original copy of John's most famous poem, "Ode on a Grecian Urn." To find the original would be astonishing. It would be worth a fortune both because it's the poet's most famous ode and because there is no original copy in John's own hand. Its worth was beyond my calculation, if it really did exist. There was also George's insistence that though everyone thought him penniless, he'd actually secreted away a fortune.

An inestimable literary artifact and a fortune. I'd have to spend more time with the journal; that was clear.

But not at the moment. I couldn't keep my eyes open one second more, so I stood and stretched, feeling both exhausted and exhilarated. I took Albert's big head in

26

my hands, kissed my favorite soft place on his muzzle, and headed for bed wondering what in the heck the Keats brothers had to do with Gray Burke and the doings going on just over the river in Bluegrass heaven.

4

I didn't see Gray for a few weeks. Understandable given the loss of Schism had cut Gray's breakout stallions in half. That and his breeding schedule meant he was much more busy than I. He'd hardly had time to think about his mother's painting. He had kept in touch, though, and when I'd asked, he mentioned the foal deaths had stopped and the vet's exam showed Schism's death had most likely been from natural causes. Being suspicious by nature, I didn't buy it. But hey, what I knew about Gray's world could fit on the head of a pin, so when it came up, I bit my tongue.

The first nice Saturday we were both free, Gray asked if I would mind coming down to the farm since his mother wanted to meet me and see if there was anything she could contribute to authenticating the painting. Gray picked me up in the Navigator, whisked me over the Ohio River and into the land of bluegrass and blue blood.

On the drive, I brought up the foals and Schism's death. Gray deftly changed the subject. Ok, I thought. When he's ready to talk, he will.

I was surprisingly happy to return to Brookfield. The rural peacefulness and beautiful horses were appealing, not to mention my nosiness about the Keats connection. I'd given the Burke painting to Alex McCafferty at the Horschow to authenticate but kept the journal to myself. At some point I'd let him look, but not touch. *Perhaps* I'd let him look. I'd become proprietary about the Keats' journal and letters.

Once on the farm we headed over the rise behind the barns to the home of Lillian Burke, Gray's mother, and the stately whitewashed, red brick colonial where Gray and his sister had grown up. As we rounded the circular drive and stopped, Gray paused.

"There's something you ought to know before we go in," he said. He had on the ubiquitous khakis and a light blue oxford shirt with the Brookfield logo. A ball cap sat on the back seat. He smelled clean like new hay, or what I imagined new hay might smell like.

"Remember Brett?" Gray was talking. "The fellow who takes care of the stallions for me?"

I nodded.

"Brett's my cousin. His father and my mother were brother and sister."

Well, ok. Not sure why the clarification was needed, especially since the two of them couldn't be more different—Gray polished and with that relaxed masculinity and Brett lanky and unkempt. Had I not known, I never would have guessed they were related.

He sighed. "My mother is really touchy about the family situation. She wants to be helpful, but she feels really uncomfortable talking about family business. Especially with Brett going on all the time about this cigar box he's got that he thinks has clues to something. Anyway, I thought you should know how sensitive she is about the family history before you meet her." His smile broadened. "We are a bit complex."

I could certainly sympathize with a woman as private as Lillian seemed to be. I valued my privacy just as highly. And then it dawned on me. Gray was also a Keats.

"So you're a Keats? Brett's a Keats?"

He nodded. "Here a Keats, there a Keats . . . ."

Well, well, well. It made sense now why the Audubon print was in the Burke family. And the Keats journal.

And of course, I was very interested in seeing the contents of Brett's cigar box. I'd only gotten to read the Keats journal through once, not study it as I wanted to. But if Brett felt he had "clues" to something, I wondered if they comported with what was in the journal.

I'd done a little research into George, especially his death. The public record states he died bankrupt—actually it states he amounted to little more than the family mooch—but his journal clearly suggested he'd secreted away some sort of fortune. Maybe Brett's box contained clues to that. Or to the whereabouts of the ode.

"So where's Brett's dad now?" I asked, mostly to keep Gray talking.

"It's a convoluted story," said Gray. "My mother got along fine with her father—the one who lived at the Seelbach Hotel over in Louisville, but Brett's dad . . . he was the black sheep of the family, I guess. He never got along with his dad, never went to visit him—but Brett and the old man were very close. We were all happy that Brett had some sort of father, since his own dad was pretty much out of the picture. Anyway, as the story goes, the old man and my dad's father were buddies, even though my dad's family settled in Lexington and the Keats side of the family was in Louisville. I heard it was gambling that got my dad's father over to Louisville, but who knows. Anyhow, they were friends, which is how my mother met my dad in the first place."

Gray paused a moment, eying me. I wasn't bored in the least if that's what he wondered. I blinked but said nothing. He continued.

"Some people think these old guys had a business arrangement, but since nobody ever saw my Grandpa at the Seelbach work, that's sort of a mystery. Anyhow, Brett was more or less abandoned by his father, and it's a touchy thing with my mother. So when his dad passed, Brett was left out in the cold—so he came to live here with us. And since he'd grown so much, he couldn't really make it as a jockey. I guess what I'm trying to say is, he's just always going to have a place here with us."

Gray stopped again and peered at me to see if any of this made sense.

"I get it," I said. "You all could be a mini-series."

Gray laughed. "Yeah, at the very least."

Lillian greeted us at the door. She was big-boned but refined in a Southern sort of way. She was delicate yet sturdy, with ash brown hair streaked heavily with silver in the front. She wore it swept back from her face and piled in a loose French roll. She had the clear green eyes she'd bestowed on her son and, though she was a solid, tall woman, her arms had thinned and her hands were freckled, whether from age or the sun I couldn't tell. I had a difficult time pinpointing her age; maybe mid-fifties, maybe somewhat older.

She stood momentarily at the opened red door. I stared at her as she smiled patiently back at me. Once inside, we passed by the dining room and into the formal living room done in enough yellow and pink chintz to choke the life out of an *Architectural Digest* cover.

She was clearly fond of Gray; she gave him space, but you couldn't be with them both and not feel the mutual affection and respect they had for one another. It was a very comfortable relationship, one I frankly envied.

"Would you care for some raspberry lemonade?" she asked me. "It's early in the year for it, but it's sort of a specialty of mine."

The incongruity of the sliver of snow on the ground and a summery beverage made me consider briefly if the woman was senile. However, she smiled, Gray smiled, and we had drinks all around. I found her admiration of the lemonade well-founded.

Lillian turned to me and handed over a tiled drink coaster. "I'm so pleased you agreed to make another trip down to the farm." She placed her hands in her lap and glanced in Gray's direction as if to get the conversation started.

We chatted about the horses, what I'd thought of the stallions, how I enjoyed living in Cincinnati, whether or not I'd come to the races, and then we all fell silent.

Lillian set down her glass and asked if I'd had any news of her "sketch."

I looked blankly at Gray. "'Sketch' is what Audubon called his paintings."

"That's what I was told it was," said Lillian, "when I inherited it."

There the conversation seemed to stall. I thought Lillian wanted to give me some information about the "sketch."

"I turned it over to our art department," I began, "but if you have any information that might help authenticate it—any history or information about its provenance?" I prompted her.

"Well, they were handed down to me," said Lillian. "The sketch and the journal came together. I was told that George Keats had received the sketch as a gift from Audubon. You see George and his wife lived with the Audubons, right here in Kentucky, when they first arrived from England."

That's what the journal indicated, too. I nodded, hoping she'd continue.

"They had a very rough time of it, as you might imagine. Kentucky was more or less frontier at that time. Very rough. Many unscrupulous people took advantage of the newcomers. Some were old Revolutionary war veterans, some were downright swindlers. There were no cities to speak of, no culture of course." Lillian paused here to take a sip. She was staying far away from any real information about her family.

"But Audubon's wife was from the East," she said, "and had some lovely things, I've heard. She made George and his wife feel very much at home. They lived in a log cabin and had a pet turkey, so the story goes."

I would have loved to hear more about the early days of Kentucky, but I was most interested in information that might help Alex authenticate the painting.

"Do you have any information about the circumstances under which Audubon gave the painting, sorry, 'sketch,' to George Keats?"

Lillian thought a moment. "No, other than the journal which you have."

I sighed. I wasn't sure why Lillian had asked me to make the trip; I hadn't learned anything of much use to Alex. The "sketch" was beautiful. I'd taken a peek before turning it over; it was a delicate, subtly colored painting of a lovely set of swans. All but one were running forward on the ice or in some state of leaping and flying into the air at a very early hour, given the rosy color of the sky. And all were white, excepting one black swan that remained on the ice, its graceful neck curved back over its plumage, its head resting on its back.

"Mrs. Burke," I began, and she waved at me.

"Oh, call me Lillian," she said. "We don't stand on ceremony here."

Of course not. They were refined but not stuffy, polite without that stereotypical Southern saccharine sweetness. I told her I hadn't heard anything yet, but I'd let her know the minute I did.

I felt perplexed as we stood to leave; I hadn't gained one ounce of information I hadn't had already. Except that the Audubons had a pet turkey.

With that, Gray and I left to take the tour of the stallion barn—the tour that had been cut short by Schism's death on my previous trip—and to watch one of them breed. And that was how I inserted myself into the Burke family and how I came to participate in the deadly events that followed.

5

March had at last passed wildly away, and we were into a mild early April. As we drove toward the office and barns, I couldn't help but think T.S. Eliot had got it all wrong. April was not the "cruelest month," as he'd said, at least not around these flowery parts.

But in fact T.S. Eliot had it right. This April would be the cruelest month, but at that moment in the mild air and gentle sunshine, I could hardly have imagined the events taking shape just over the horizon.

What I could see was the strain Gray was under, once we'd left his mother's house and there was no need to put on a good show for her. I wondered if it had to do with the deaths or if something else was weighing on him.

This was Gray's busy season—most of the mares foaled, others shipped in to breed and either stayed or were shipped back to their owners. There were also the boarders to be foaled and bred. So March and April, he said, were generally a blur.

When we arrived at Gray's office, a fat man was standing in the gravel, hands on hips, scowling at the Navigator. I looked questioningly at Gray; he shoved the shift into park and hopped out. Immediately they were in some heated discussion, with the fat guy poking his fat finger up at Gray's face. My initial reaction was negative. He was not happy and neither was Gray. I wanted to roll down the window, but that would be too obvious. I heard bits and pieces, but not enough to get the gist. In a moment, Gray turned on his heel and headed over to my window.

"I hate to do this, Julia," he said as I inched it down. He leaned in, and I could tell how agitated he was; it didn't show on his face, but it did in his eyes. "Would you mind if I talked to Horace a few minutes in private?"

Ah, Horace Laroveneur. The partner, of sorts.

Gray glanced back at Horace's hefty presence. "It won't take long," he said, biting off the words.

"Of course," I said. He seemed anxious as well as agitated, and I wondered what that was all about. "I'll head to the stallion complex and meet you at the breeding shed."

I watched Gray and Horace walk into the building, presumably to scream and yell at each other in the confines of Gray's office. I walked through the cemetery and on to the stallion complex. It was fair weather and the flower beds along the path were blooming: large stands of budded purple lavender arched up next to bush peonies in pink and white. I came across the bridge and I stopped in front of a fountain shooting up water in alternating heights and sat on the hand-fitted fieldstones set with plaques at intervals around it. Each was for a Brookfield stallion—its birth and death dates were there along with the horse's greatest hits: Blue Note's plaque read, "Horse of the Year," and then a date. There were a lot of plaques. Gray had plenty to lose.

There were also a lot of live stallions. To the right and left stood eight small, wooden barns amid tall oaks and spreading maples. Each held four large stalls, I knew, marked by two windows each, plus a long thin window at a horse's head height. Thirty-two stallions could live on the farm. Behind these structures, a large, low-roofed, blue, corrugated-metal exercise building stood open to the air. To the right was the breeding shed—a very tall building with lots of windows set in the roofline; as I stood facing it, the large door stood open to a wide central, dirt-floored aisle flanked by more stalls. The building angled off to the right where there looked to be even more stalls and another doorway through which a few olive-skinned young men were just leaving.

The stallion barns were neat and well cared for as was the entire farm, with a red brick walkway running around the base of each structure, a hand-laid stone foundation topped by wood siding, and long peaked roofs. Each had a large wood planked door on wrought iron rollers at the top to open and close the barn. It was oddly quiet.

I headed toward the first barn and Richard, the South African stallion manager, met me on the gravel. He was dragging three rakes laced together, making a neat swirling pattern on the walkway.

"Hi," I said, "I'm Julia."

Richard nodded and kept up his work. He was powerfully built with a strong upper body. "Yeah," he said in his clipped South African accent, "I know . . . Chance breeds at two." he said and walked off, dragging the linked rakes behind him. He was friendly, but clearly all about minding his own business, though he certainly seemed to know enough about mine.

I passed into the first barn, going from light into its cool, dim interior.

It was still and quiet inside the barn, but for the overhead fans. I looked in at the back end of Antienne, as the plaque outside his stall read, nudging aside the old hay to munch on new green alfalfa. He didn't seem to notice my presence.

Behind me, Circuit Breaker walked over and gazed

at me through the ornate bars. He was a gleaming dark brown, very large stallion with big brown eyes and a bit of blue in the center. He angled his head and licked the bars with a fat pink tongue.

"What is he doing?" I said to the groom who'd walked in—an older, slim, neat man in blue jeans heading for the other end of the barn.

"He just wants attention," he said, like that's unusual in a caged animal.

I looked back at the horse. He continued licking and kept his eye on me. I could easily reach in and scratch his forehead, but remembered Gray mentioning fingers being nipped off, so I just said, "What do you do when he acts like this?"

"Me?" said the man and laughed in a dismissive way, "I just walk on by. Give 'em attention, and that's all they want."

I reached out and scratched Circuit Breaker's forehead just over the white blaze.

He went on licking, but his ear had turned to me. He had a kind eye, so I moved down to his soft muzzle and continued. The horse kept his angled eye on me and licked the bars.

I moved down the row and looked in on a smaller horse, a bay; across from him was an empty stall. I walked out into the sunlight and headed around the barn to the next one. I wasn't looking for Medes' stall, but I wouldn't avoid it if I happened upon it.

"You shouldna loved on him," the groom called after me from the shadows of the barn doorway. He was sarcastic and I didn't like him.

I walked back in.

"He seen you out the back window," said the man and pointed at Circuit Breaker who had swung his head back from the window and now made his way to the bars where I stood to resume his licking. "Looks like he don't wancha ta leave, darlin'."

I stuck my hand through the bar and scratched the blaze.

"Told ye," he said. His tone suggested only a dope "coddled" the horses.

Just then Gray came striding across the gravel. "Here you are."

Coming alongside me he absently rubbed the horse's muzzle and was quiet. He looked stressed.

I asked about the groom too stingy to give a horse even a pat, and it's likely I didn't hide my distaste.

Gray glanced toward the doorway. "That's Chaney. He covers if someone's off or sick. He sort of takes up the slack. Also helps shipping out the stallions for the season in . . ." Gray looked at me, assessing my tone. He frowned and folded his arms. "South America . . . He's been around a long time," he said, challenging the conclusion I'd drawn about the groom. I suppose my face gave me away.

"Obviously," I said. I still didn't like Chaney no matter how long he'd been around or how helpful he was to the farm.

"Getting these boys ready for travel is no small job. Chaney knows his stuff, and I'm glad to have him," said Gray, further defending the groom.

I asked where the stallions were shipping to.

"After they stand our season," he said, moving smoothly behind me, taking my elbow, trying to lead me away from the stall. I stood my ground. "Some of them cover another season down in Argentina, Chile, or some might go to Australia . . . those breeders looking for new bloodlines. Antienne goes to Australia this year."

"Where is Circuit Breaker going?" I asked, not moving from his stall.

Gray reached in to play with the horse's mouth,

lifting his big lip to show his tattoo, his yellowed teeth. "Good boy," murmured Gray.

"He's going to Argentina . . . But he's not coming back."

It was warm in the barn with a soft movement of air from the overhead fans in each stall, and for the next several minutes, only the low whir from the fans was heard.

"Syndicate sold him."

I didn't say anything.

"I own part of him," said Gray and pulled his hand out. His statements seemed pretty flat to me, not full of the attachment I'd assumed between him and the stallions.

"Why don't you keep him here then?" I said with a slight edge.

Gray again was matter-of-fact. "It's not all my decision. I didn't syndicate him; Horace owns most of him, like he does Aury. I just own a little piece. And I get a foal by him every year."

Horace again. Horace of the fat fingers seemed to have them in a lot of stuff around the farm. Gray moved his head to the side and indicated we should walk on. I glanced around to see the groom sliding open the door to the empty stall.

"Getting rid of him is the right decision," he said. "His stud fee leveled out and it isn't increasing."

Something struggled toward the surface, alighted momentarily in Gray's eyes then was gone. I interpreted it as regret, but I might have been reading in my own feelings. "His first crop performed all right. After that, he held his own; he's just not attracting quality mares. I think we only booked 8 mares this season." He stopped a moment. "He might get a new start in Argentina, it might be the best thing for him."

The unspoken tension between us became more tangible; we moved closer together then apart as we headed toward the fountain.

"Well, if he's doing ok, why send him away?" I said. Gray paused on the curved gravel that Richard had so recently groomed.

"Look around," he said. "We've got close to three-hundred acres here. Mares and foals, horses in training . . . later we'll have the weanlings and yearlings to deal with besides the stallions. Once we had over twenty stallions standing at stud."

I could sense this was an argument he'd had with himself before.

"Did you meet Gavin?"

I hadn't, though I knew he was one of the stallion grooms working with Richard.

"Gavin's lived on this farm since he was five years old."

We sat on the stone around the fountain.

Gray looked at the gravel. "This is a business. We have production mares and our crops. That's the way of it. If I don't treat it that way, all my Gavins won't have a job or a place to live."

I understood. And I had sympathy. I didn't envy Gray the position he was in. But there was the issue of the foals—Gray had studiously avoided talking about their losses, in this context or any other one.

I broached the subject. "Have you figured out what might be causing your foals to die?"

Gray looked more serious. "Tim, my vet, he's looked into it but hasn't found the cause." He sighed. "If there is one. I guess the good news is, I haven't had any go down since the last time you were here. Maybe they've let up."

I hoped he was right. Maybe it was just my paranoia. Maybe Gray was right and it was just bad luck. What did I know?

He turned to the fountain. "My dad had this

designed. He liked these plaques." Gray ran his hand over Nine Lives and his deeds—another high-dollar purse winner.

I nodded. Again, he'd changed the subject. A breeze went through my hair and ended up in the row of poplars.

"All these guys did their best for us. It's a heritage, something to preserve and build on."

He looked troubled. "That's what it's supposed to be. "He glanced at the water. "That's how it's supposed to work."

I fell silent, trapped between Keats' intangible world of death and art and the vitality of Gray's world, a world in jeopardy but one I could only skirt on the periphery.

"And it isn't?" I said.

He big shoulders slumped forward in an attitude of subjection. "We lost *so* many foals when MRLS hit." He turned away from the fountain. "A lot of farms got hit hard, I'm not complaining."

Gray motioned to the empty stallion barns. "We had to sell off a lot of stock. Which was ok, this business has its ups and downs. Everyone knows that. And then this year hasn't started off so well."

I couldn't think of what to say. The looming responsibility of Brookfield—its tradition, its employees, its horses—the many lives at stake, seemed an oppressive presence to me. Gray looked on steadily, though directly, at the problems he faced.

"And we were better off than some that year," he said, picking a pinkish bit of gravel and rolling it between his fingers. "Horace has been around the block. He didn't panic."

I leaned toward him. Then slowly I said, "So you kept his mares?"

"Most of them. He wasn't as skittish as a lot of

them."

A few moments later, Brett strolled up with a box under one arm and a long hose under the other.

I saw the box nearly before I saw him.

"Afternoon," he said to us, nodding as he passed.

"Brett," said Gray and shifted positions. They did not seem comfortable at all with one another.

"What's he doing with the vacuum hose?" I said. I hadn't noticed any carpet in the barn.

"He'll groom his stallions. Gets the dust out pretty well." Gray sat by the fountain and crossed his leg over his knee.

Oh, I see. Of course, vacuum the horses.

It felt good to turn my attention to something else; there was a lot of tension in the air. I wondered when I'd be able to have a word with Brett, get his view on this illustrious family. I also wondered if Gray would like to drop the subject he'd been having some difficulty talking about.

I sat next to him, quiet in the sun, waiting out whether or not he would continue.

After an uncomfortable few moments he took my elbow and eased me to my feet.

"Let's walk if you don't mind," he said.

We headed to the left of the complex, and Gray hopped up on the rail fence encircling Aury's paddock. The chestnut stallion stood next to the fence a long stone's throw away, beneath the tall sycamore just beginning to leaf out, grazing quietly in the light.

"Horace has been a good friend. Even offered to buy me out."

"Really," I said. What was he up to is what I actually wondered. I pictured that fat finger poking at Gray's face and wondered if that's what they'd argued about. "Are things that bad?"

Gray squinted and looked out over the pastures to the long hand-laid, stone wall running the length of Paris Pike.

"Well, you know we haven't come back financially . . . yet." He thought. "Horace's offer is something to consider." He didn't look thrilled by the idea.

Gray glanced at his watch. It was nearly two o'clock.

"Did you want to see Chance breed?" he said, hopping off the fence. He put the conversation behind him. He was very good at that. "He is a very professional stallion, very well-mannered."

"Sure," I said. Out of the corner of my eye, I saw Brett come out of the barn and wave to me.

I told Gray I'd meet him in the breeding shed. Maybe I could finally get a look at that box. "I just want to look in on Circuit Breaker one more time," I lied. It's not something I do frequently. Only when necessary, I tell myself.

Gray put his hands in his pockets, and headed off. "Don't be too long. With Chance, it's over pretty quick."

I watched his back then turned to Brett. He motioned me inside the barn and followed me in.

He was sweating though the day was mild and the fans were effective. "I've been wanting to talk to you," he said and pushed back his hair. He was taller than me by a head and very thin. "Gray says you're a school teacher."

Well, that's one way to describe it. "Yes."

"And that you know all about our kin." His eyes were the color of river rock, clear brown with green and gold flecks, his face long, his hands bony. He continued to work as we talked, rearranging the tack in the small alcove at the middle of the barn.

"The Keats."

He nodded; his movements were efficient and casual born of long familiarity with the tasks. "I got a notion about my great-grandfather."

Brett inhaled deeply, which seemed to relax him a little, and kept working. He did seem overly anxious under the circumstances.

"What sort of a notion?"

He sat on the tack box, reached forward to grab a thick, stiff brush. "I'm not exactly sure. I don't know. That's why I was wanting to talk to you."

He put down the brush and knotted his hands. The horses in the barn began to nicker and whinny.

"Brett, is something bothering you?" I said, and instantly wished I hadn't. Brett reacted defensively.

He got up and took a halter from the wall hook. "What would I have to be bothered about?"

He glanced at the open doorway as if checking for someone. Then, satisfied that we were alone, he continued. "My grandpa died a while back, and I got this parcel of stuff of his. I been going through it, and I found this key." He pulled a small, flat, brass-looking key out of his pocket.

"So I found out it was from a bank, and I went and it was a safety deposit box. Inside was another box."

I sat down beside him. A key, then a box, then another box. Puzzle inside a puzzle. He didn't resume his seat and again glanced out the door then back toward the other opening.

"What was in the box, Brett?"

"Well, that's it. I'm not sure. There's a drawing in there and it looks real old."

Another drawing . . . Another Audubon "sketch"? I glanced at the box. A pretty small one if it fit in there. I looked at my watch. I didn't have a lot of time to spend with Brett or I'd miss the breeding.

"What do you think this has to do with your relative?" I said. Or me, I thought, but truthfully I was intrigued.

"Well, there's a paper that's signed 'Samuel Keats.' Now that's my great-granddad. And his pappy was George Keats who come over here from England."

"What does the paper say?"

"You could see it, I got it with me . . . It says some things I can't figure. I got it and all the other stuff right here." He looked imploringly at me.

At the mention of George Keats, of course, I wanted to see everything that box contained. But I would miss the breeding if I lingered much longer. I felt I'd better join Gray as I'd promised. "I have to meet Gray in a minute, but can you tell me anything about what it says?"

"Well, there's something about keeping a secret. It's confusing."

"Have you spoken with Gray about this?" It seemed he should be talking to his cousin about this, not me. "Or your aunt?" I asked, thinking there must be someone closer to him to help puzzle this out. Though, of course, I intended also to be involved. After spending time with his journal, I'd grown oddly close to George Keats in the last month. I wasn't about to sit on the sidelines.

"Yes, I told him about this here box I keep all of it in," Brett showed me the box he had secreted in the closet to his left. "Aunt Lillian, though, she don't care to talk much about it. Gray neither. But that's when I come to find out about you being a teacher."

Brett looked even more befuddled, and he was still sweating. "I'm just not sure what it all means, but it was important to my grand-pa that I get it, which is why he put it in that box at the bank."

"Would you like me to take a look at all of it sometime?"

Brett seemed astonished. "Would you do that?"

I rose. "Sure. I'd be happy to."

"Now?" he said, glancing around. "I don't let

anyone take ahold of it but me."

"How about next time I come? I'll tell Gray to let you know."

He seemed relieved, childlike, and was content with my offer.

"We'll look it over together," I said. He looked so grateful, I was torn about leaving. He walked me out as far as the barn door.

I entered the breeding shed thinking over what Brett had said. I really had to see his artifacts and had already started mentally planning another trip to Brookfield sometime soon. First, though, I wanted more information about the discrepancies between the public and private record of George Keats.

Just ahead of me was a black-padded chute in which stood a bay mare getting her tail wrapped with white, gauzy tape. Gray stood chatting with his vet, Tim Bradford. He let the man get back to his perusal of the mare's rear end and joined me, letting Gavin finalize the mare's tail wrap, which prevented her wiry hair cutting Serious Chances where he least needed it.

"She's ready," called Tim and the mare was backed out of the chute.

We passed into a thirty-foot, three-story open room with an elevated office to the right, a curved viewing stand before it, and in the center, a black padded seven-by-five foot wall around which was laid a sixteen-foot square hard-rubber surface. The breeding would take place there. The rest of the room was floored with wood chips and every other surface was covered in ten-inch black padding.

"Step up?" said Gray and we stood behind the padded viewing platform. A small Brazilian man stepped in next to us.

"Big room," I said. To the right was a fifteen-foot high curved wall just adjacent to the open door facing the stallion barns.

"That's for safety. Ours and the horses'."

The mare was led in from the left, and Tim Bradford went into the office behind us. Soon he was out again and up at the padded breeding stand, the breeding roll in his hand.

"Excuse me," said Gray and went to the wall where he took down a leather shield; its presence provided the stallion with purchase rather than have him bite into the back of a million dollar mare. Gray laid it over the mare as the groom twitched her lip. Her eyes rolled a bit and she stood calmly.

Serious Chances was the 16.3-hand gray stallion I'd met in the stallion barn. He was led in on a leather and chain shank by Manuel, his groom, who whisked him behind the high partition to wash him off.

A groom by the mare's head bent her left front leg and wrapped it up in a leather strap, holding it there so she'd be off-balance and wouldn't kick the stallion.

"Turn her tail," said Gray, as Richard appeared suddenly and Tim took the mare's wrapped tail and held it off her right flank as Chance was led around the partition. Immediately the stallion's head came up. He flared his nostrils, barred his teeth, and called to the mare. His neck arched, his tail drew high, and he pranced in place. Manuel gave a pull on the shank to get his attention. Chance nodded his head up and down, uttering guttural sounds that caused the mare to try to turn her head.

The twitch prevented that.

Now Gavin and another groom moved to the mare's flank to steady her; Gray stood on the other side with Tim. Richard took the stallion's shank from Manuel who had led him up to the mare. She sidestepped once and then Chance reared up and came down on her back, his neck arching over her, his head bent to the breeding shield, already beginning to thrust. The groom let the mare's near leg go. Manuel guided Chance into the mare just as Tim Bradford placed the breeding roll between her and the stallion, preventing him penetrating her too deeply.

The room was completely quiet.

In less than a minute, after a few thrusts and low gutturals, Serious Chances flared his tail, backed off, and calmly dropped to the ground. The small man next to me said, "He know his business," and pulled on his ball cap. Three grooms backed the stallion around the partition to be washed once again. He complied without comment.

Manuel handed the Styrofoam cup in which he'd collected the last of Chance's semen as he'd dismounted and Tim took it to the office where he looked at a sample under the microscope.

I turned to watch him, and after assuring himself that there were motile sperm, he raised the cup to me.

"Cheers," I said and he laughed.

Gray came over and helped me down as the mare was led out on the opposite side of the room from Chance.

"Got to keep them apart," said Richard as he passed, stripping off his shoulder-length plastic sleeves.

We watched the mare go into the chute, and soon Tim was standing in back of her inserting a thin tube. His arm was sheathed in the same type of plastic sleeve up to his shoulder as Richard had worn, and within a few seconds it had disappeared nearly up to the elbow. The mare seemed unconcerned, glancing around only once. Tim injected the syringe of Serious Chance's "extended" semen into the mare.

"Hope we got her," he said, withdrawing his arm and stripping off the sleeve.

He walked around to the mare's head and slapped her neck affectionately. "Do a good job, now," he said to her.

Gray stood at my side. "She will, doc. She always does."

I counted: It took seven or eight men to breed the stallion. That's a lot of mouths to feed. In addition to the horses.

6

To my great annoyance, once back home my university workload picked up so I couldn't get back down to Brookfield as soon as I'd hoped. Not only were there my classes, but work at the classics library had also increased coincident with our acquisition of nineteenth century periodicals. I work my own schedule there—as long I get my work done, no one monitors my hours. Unfortunately, at the moment, eighteenth- and nineteenth-century consumer publications were all the rage in academia. Consequently, coffee house gossip as published in the weeklies kept me busy cataloguing, examining, describing, and otherwise babysitting them for more time than I liked, and I couldn't break away until my work was finished.

I hadn't mentioned my conversation with Brett to Gray so I couldn't very well ask him to tell Brett I'd return as soon as I could. I just had to stew in my own juices, hoping my delay hadn't spoiled Brett's eagerness to share the contents of his box. Adding to my frustration was the fact that I'd had very little time to work on the Keats' journal; but from the limited research I'd been able to do, I had pieced together a few interesting facts.

I knew that there were letters from John to George

and from George to John that were known to have been written but were not in any collections; they were presumed lost. Second, a favor called in had verified that both the loose sheets and the journal were authentic. But while I had sure knowledge that the loose sheets were in John Keats' hand, I had no conclusive verification that the journal entries were written by George, though I was sure they had been.

I clamored for more information, and I knew that it resided in Louisville. I'd been waiting to visit the Filson Historical Society library there since it housed original materials on the George Keats family, and the next week Gray made that visit more appealing.

"Want to meet me at the Seelbach Hotel?" he said over the phone late one Thursday evening.

Well, that is quite a proposition, I thought. Then I realized his offer was likely much less racy than my interpretation of it.

I'd stayed at the Seelbach once while delivering a paper at the University of Louisville—a struggling assistant professor sleeping in a lofty four-poster bed. The hotel is one of the city's historical landmarks, a gracious and baroque structure with period reproductions in the rooms. F. Scott Fitzgerald had been so struck by the Seelbach, he'd fashioned Daisy Buchanan's "Great Gatsby" wedding using the hotel as a backdrop. It had hosted Taft and Roosevelt, among other presidents through the years, had an entire banquet room done in original Rookwood pottery, and Kentucky's only triple A-rated restaurant. I relished the idea of returning. And to boot, the Filson was only a few miles from the hotel. Albert was due to attend a show with his breeder for the weekend so he was spoken for.

"I love the Seelbach," I said.

"Great. Horace and his wife are staying there and they'd like to have a meeting." Gray paused, then continued with less enthusiasm. "Some of the other syndicate members will be there, too. I think they want to talk to me about the . . . situation." Gray paused. "I hoped you might like to come along." He had to wait only a minute for me to accept the offer.

We agreed to meet for dinner Friday with the Laroveneurs, then Saturday, part ways—Gray to the syndicate meeting, and I would head down the road to the Filson.

Friday evening, after shimmying into my little black dress, I headed downstairs to meet Gray and the Laroveneurs for drinks and dinner in the Seelbach's Oakroom. The lobby was generously sized and lit by two enormous hanging chandeliers, which reflected softly against the muted murals circling the upper portion of the walls. Shining cream and deep green marble accented by scrolled gilt covered the rest of the walls and pillars. I crossed to the central staircase curving upward before me and flanked by gilt banisters topped by full-length portraits of two ladies, one on either side of the landing. To the right was The Oakroom's lounge, a carpeted, dark-paneled room where I was to meet everyone for drinks before dinner. The atmosphere was Kentucky gentility at its finest.

"Well, here she is," called Horace, hefting his Kentucky bourbon neat in my direction, as I made my way across to the three of them. A waiter pulled my chair out, and I sat at the low coffee table to the right of Gray, ordering a California chardonnay and settling in for drinks before dinner.

Gray introduced me to Miriam, Horace's wife, who looked me over as if I was an item on the menu. She likely was once lovely; her thick, dark hair was pulled back in a chignon that drew attention to her high cheekbones and squared jaw. Her dark blue eyes contrasted with fair skin under which tiny veins showed at the temple. Miriam was unreadable.

Horace, however, was something of an ass.

As waiters circulated, balancing drinks on round cork-topped trays and the lounge admitted patrons in dresses, suits, and lots of jewelry, Horace leaned back in his leather chair.

"So, little missy," he said to me, "what do you think of our horse bidness?"

I was nonplussed by the coupling of "missy" with "bidness," so Gray jumped in. "She's taken a liking to Circuit Breaker, Horace," he said mildly, "and from what I saw, the feeling is mutual."

"Heh-heh," said Horace.

I noticed Miriam was surveying the lounge. She glanced up and a waiter came quickly. She nodded at him for another drink; that seemed all that was necessary.

"Well," he said, "it comes as no surprise. No surprise et-all. That stallion has always had good taste. Heh-heh . . . Too bad good taste don't translate into good runners." He trailed off and sipped his drink.

I looked up at the small, gold-framed picture of a man on horseback on the wall behind us. Gray turned the talk in a different direction. "Miriam's family has been in the horse business longer than mine." He smiled at Miriam as if asking her to take up the topic but Horace spoke instead.

"Her father and his father before him, and back on into Ireland—they was all trainers and breeders." He grabbed the back of Miriam's chair and leaned over to her but looked at me. "Miriam's pappy trained all Gray's daddy's runners." He raised his glass to Gray. "We are a happy family here . . . we certainly are."

He put down his glass and leaned back, smiling proprietarily at Miriam. "Ye might say we made a dy*nast*ic union, me and Miriam. My horse sense and her, uh . . .

connections."

Miriam smiled what in former years might have been termed "demurely" but now seemed more than slight embarrassment. Miriam sipped her Cosmopolitan discreetly and said nothing.

I felt sure the only "sense" Horace had had was to marry well.

The hostess approached to say our table was ready. We trailed her into the dining room and were seated to the left of the entrance. We ordered soon after: T-bone for Horace, Blue-Grass chicken stuffed with country ham for Miriam, Kentucky rack of lamb with black truffle sauce for Gray, and (as the menu noted) "A Study of Crab" for me. We also ordered two wines suggested by the sommelier—a white and a red. All was accompanied by The Oakroom's sour-mash-bourbon bread, and when it was served, everything was delicious.

"So," said Horace, pointing his beef-speared fork at Gray following the service of our entrées, "I am serious about breedin' my Imperial Quest to that Aury of ours. Dead serious. We're gonna get a great one outa her, I can feel it." He chewed and looked to Gray for confirmation.

"Well, I can see your point," began Gray, but Horace interrupted, addressing me.

"You see, little lady," he began, chewing and bending over his plate, "bein' successful," and here he glanced at Gray, "depends on knowin' how to get a well-made foal. That's whut this game is all about." He smiled. "A well-made foal will sell."

Miriam smiled at me. It was the first human gesture she'd made since I'd sat down.

"Horace, dear," she said, and lightly placed a hand on his forearm. "Julia may not be interested at all in you conducting business over dinner." She smiled at me again. Distantly, but it was a start.

"No, no," I said, "I'm fascinated. Really." I was actually interested.

Horace humphed. "Or run. Ye ken sell or run a horse like that. Ye look to get a horse that gives ye options." He gulped his red wine. "Me," he said, wiping his mouth, "I prefer colts . . . To sell. Now I'll take a filly at Keeneland now an again."

Horace scraped the potatoes he'd emptied from the skin into a heap, salted it heavily, and dug in, then took another swig of wine.

I looked away.

"It's not just the sales," said Gray smoothly, "when a stallion retires to stud you don't know how he'll do as a sire. Some stallions don't do well at the track but have a good pedigree—that's Aury. He didn't do much as a runner, cracked a sesamoid, retired early, but his offspring are running well. So he's maybe a better sire than a racehorse."

Horace said, "Best if they ken do both."

"Right," agreed Gray.

Horace said to Gray. "It would certainly not sit well for you to be forced into sellin' off on ole Aury." He forked in a mouthful. "Wouldn't be fittin'."

The air turned suddenly chilly.

"But then, that's whut friends are for," he said, pausing to look at Gray, "should it come to that." He smiled at me, and resumed eating.

Miriam studied her chicken as if she hadn't heard her husband's crass comments.

There was an awkward silence filled with a tension born of Gray's financial difficulties.

I forked crab into my mouth and chewed. Miriam looked on impassively. There was a prolonged, uncomfortable silence.

"Ye see that room over there," Horace said, finally.

I looked at where he'd pointed; it was a private

dining room with a chandelier and long, rectangular table set for a party of twelve.

"That's Al Capone's room," he continued. "Gentlemen used to come in here to gamble." He gestured to the large dining room. "Truly." He nodded at his own veracity. "And in that room over there were the serious gamblers."

Gray agreed. "That's right. Al Capone used to come here and head straight to that room. F. Scott Fitzgerald spent time here, too. History has it, he was kicked out one evening after having a bit too much to drink." Gray toasted to F. Scott's memory. His tone suggested relief at moving from the nuances of the previous conversation.

"Yes, and there's a secret in there," said Horace, returning to Al Capone's room. "A secret staircase, two of 'em really, one of 'em leading to fourth street and the other goes the other way."

Gray looked at me and smiled as if to say Horace was really quite harmless. Just an old storyteller.

It did not, however, seem so to me.

Horace continued. "This was so when the cops raided, they'd have a way to excape. Now it's boarded up, of course."

I looked at Gray, not convinced of Horace's innocuousness.

"Always good to have a excape plan," he said looking pointedly at Gray. "Always a good idea. Don't you think so, Gray?"

I looked at Gray. His eyes were no longer smiling; he seemed tired but his lips curved slightly.

"Now I think Miriam's right, Horace. Time enough to talk business tomorrow."

"Bidness?" said Horace. "Who's talking bidness? I'm speaking about ole Al Capone. Just a story for Miss Julia about that ole cutthroat gangster used to come here."

He chewed slowly, not taking his eyes off Gray.

We had wild blueberry buckle with buttermilk sorbet for desert, but I can't say I ate much of it.

The next day I got up early and drove the few miles to the Filson Historical Society, housed in the Ferguson Mansion, originally a family residence designed by the same firm that designed the Seelbach; I was as interested in the library's home as I was in its collection.

It is a beautiful structure with ornate quarter-sawn wood paneling and murals on the first floor, a recreated period sitting room on the second, and a host of portraits from the 19th and early 20th centuries throughout. These portraits captivated me; the earlier paintings of men and women, from the era George Keats first arrived in Kentucky, show the women in dark clothes and lace with grim, set faces. Those painted around or after the turn of the century show women with softer expressions and dressed in flowing gowns with elbow-length gloves; their men stare out from their erect poses with clear, direct gazes.

Nothing but confidence and success for these pillars of commerce. I scurried past them to the second floor, where I read about Audubon's early years in Kentucky. Though the 1819 failed riverboat venture that sent George Keats penniless back to England is noted, there was no mention of Keats in the Audubon biographies. No clues to the treasure on the second floor.

I did find a portrait of George, enlarged from a period miniature. It shows him a slight-shouldered, balding, finely featured man of a mild countenance. As I looked longer at this portrait, it also struck me that the nostalgic entries I'd been reading looked back at a time vastly different from the one in which he wrote. In 1810 the county's population is listed as 4,012 inhabitants. Louisville was a wilderness town, as George's experiences underline. Many men, scoundrels among them as Lillian had noted, were attracted there due to the low-priced, fertile land. There was a sizable population of Englishmen who'd also come to America to earn their fortune; as George's journal attested, it was with them that he and his young wife meant to live. By 1841, when George wrote about his experiences during those early days in Kentucky, Louisville's population had increased to 21,000.

I leafed through the photocopies I'd brought of George's journal, and found the one I was searching for—dated July 16th, 1841.

> *I am not a large man. Yet I did hope to contribute something in thanks to the gracious hospitality of the Audubons—what serendipitous fortune, I thought at the time, to have them as our hosts. I wished especially to be of service to the providential Lucy who had made our life in the wilderness much more than tolerable with her care, her enlightened conversation and vitality. So I did what little I could, not being the meat of a man that Audubon was. I chopped wood or gathered kindling, the latter, I know, not being the most manly of chores, but it was an offering of gratitude I could only hope was accepted in the spirit in which it was undertaken.*

> *Just that afternoon, upon our return from the shores of the Ohio, I thought to provide some fire wood for the evening meal. Audubon loomed over me at the chopping block to the side of the cabin, wagging his hairy head and crossing his leather-clad arms. He took pride in his great ax, which I confess, I lofted into the air with substantial effort, very unlike my host, as around*

59

me the blasted turkey honked and careened. Sweat poured from my brow. My efforts were scrutinized, and for the briefest moment I thought of happy evenings at the dance or at table among men and women of culture and breeding—an evening at Dilkes perhaps, or alone with my brother John in close and intimate conversation.

Audubon, however, shortly brought me out of this reverie.

In his coarse manner, he made attempts to instill in me no little confidence regarding my future. "Keats!" he shouted. "I am sure you will do well in this country!" I looked up momentarily to see him in serious consideration of my inept ax wielding, "For a man who will persist," he continued, "as you have been doing, in chopping that log, though it has taken you an hour to do what I would do in ten minutes, will certainly get along here."

I fervently hoped he was right.

I sat back, and looked at George's portrait, struck again by how unprepared he had been, both physically and psychologically, for his life in this new world. Accustomed to the coffee houses, drawing rooms, and theatres of London this smallish man had thrust himself into the wild interior where thievery, swindles, and strength prevailed. Audubon, as George described him, seemed literally a giant, a man of such audacity that Keats could never have hoped to match him. Audubon, at least as he seemed in George's recollection, was certainly well able to overpower, if not overshadow, the young George Keats. Yet George had overcome all these challenges, maybe even prevailed over them. And through everything I read in George's journal ran one desire —a wish to care for his family. It seemed he'd do anything to achieve that. In that way he seemed so much like Gray, a relative he could never have predicted.

My question was, did he in fact hide the treasure he referred in the journal? If so, where the heck was it?

I ventured up the steep steps to the Filson's manuscript collection in order to learn more. The dark, close stairway opened onto the darkened third floor landing. Like all original collections worthy of their Dewey-decimalesque systems, the Filson requires completing a detailed check-in form which includes your name, phone number, and address, a promise to gain official permission to use any materials therein, and on the flip side of the sheet, a listing of those documents you'd like retrieved. I also had to turn over my driver's license and leave my camera, notepaper, portfolio, and pen outside the library study room. I had already parked my purse in the lower level locker, and upon surrendering the articles it was permissible to use on the second floor, I was issued special collections paper for notes and a pencil.

I went into the study room and sat at a wide-planked table to leaf through the black cardboard box containing folders with original correspondence. It's a really good thing that the Filson closes at noon on Saturday, or I would have been there into the night since I so easily get lost in the past.

After a while, I began shuffling my feet, suddenly missing Albert; he so often accompanies my forays into the long ago, lying quietly at the foot of the couch as I work. I thought of him prancing around the ring in Indianapolis and smiled.

Over the next several hours, I plodded through primary source material *about* George Keats and his family, but there was nothing written by him or his family. It was frustrating not to find one single piece of paper written by George Keats himself; I was handed folders filled with yellowing onion skin or thick browning paper scrawled with black ink, all written by the good people of Louisville gossiping about George and his family. What a glutton I am—I had an entire diary at home in his hand and photocopies of the same in the next room, so I stopped my grousing and focused on what George's so-called friends had to say about him.

The Keatses had a lot of children and only one died early. It was Isabelle's tragedy, though, that made me a fan of George forever. His journal had a long, detailed account of her death, so I was well aware of what happened. A lovely, vivacious child, Isabelle was the fourth daughter; it wasn't until Samuel and then John Henry were born, in 1826 and 27, that the Keats family had sons to continue the family name. There would be another, Clarence George, followed by two more girls. By all accounts Isabelle was the brightest; talented in writing, happy, funny, smart, and of all the children, she was most like her famous Uncle John. At the time of her death, on October 20, 1839, she had just started writing and appeared to be the precocious American inheritor of her uncle's talent. Her life ended in her early teens, the victim of a gunshot wound about which there was speculation: was it a suicide or, as the family reported, a tragic accident? Or was she murdered?

Then there were the reports that George had died bankrupt. There was a whole lot of gossip about that in the letters—it was the *People Magazine* version of George and his family. The Louisville folk gossiped about how Georgiana was left penniless and with a lot of kids; a year later she married John Jeffrey, a man who *supposedly* admired George Keats. But Jeffrey's admiration might have resulted in him conveniently "losing" a lot of letters between George and John—why was anyone's guess. Samuel, who was 16 at the time of his father's death, was to marry and have one child. Eventually that line produced

Gray and his cousin Brett.

The journal I had was completely at odds with the report George had died bankrupt. I wondered if that was the "notion" Brett had referred to. How I wished I'd taken the time that day to look at the contents of Brett's cigar box. Now I was even more anxious to talk to him. Plus I wanted to do more research at home to find out if that lost ode I was sniffing around for could be accounted for in the published letters between George and John. Or was that one of the letters Jeffrey had "lost" for some unfathomable reason? I was kind of interested in the fortune—for Gray, I told myself. Really, for Gray and the farm. But for me, I was after the ode.

I left the Filson at the stroke of noon, turning in my badge on the first floor and retrieving my purse from the locker. Leaving the Filson was like waking up from a nineteenth-century dream. The dark, somber portraits amid dark, somber lighting gave way to the bright, cool day as I walked out the side door into the parking lot. I was anxious to get back to the Seelbach and meet Gray for lunch. He'd told me the syndicate would break around one, so I had plenty of time to go to my room, organize my notes, and review George's account of Isabelle's death.

Once in my room, I sat at the desk, stapled together the notes I'd taken on the white notepaper given me in the manuscript reading room, and set them to one side. I'd snapped a picture of George's portrait with my digital camera, and now I set the camera on the desk in front of me, flicked it on, and called up the portrait. Next I shuffled through the photocopies of George's journal until I came to his entry about the death of his daughter. I poured a glass of water and began to read.

September 17, 1841
The day dawns in a mist, or perhaps I am

up earlier than usual this day. For the first time in a long while, I'm feeling strong enough to rise, dress, even eat. I'm to breakfast with the Johnstone brothers, Mr. Clemens, and Sidney Fearing, concerning the proposal I sent them a week last. I fervently hope they see the virtues of my plan. But this has begun a difficult year and I fear. I fear it may not go well.

I still wake, thinking I hear your voice Isabelle, which I know is a natural event . . . you've not left us that long ago. Not long enough for your voice to have faded—you have been well received by your Uncle Tom, I trust, and the one whom you most resemble, our beloved John.

I have resolved to put down the events of that night in hopes it may relieve my mind. I cannot sleep well, perhaps because I cannot leave you behind. I hope the telling will aid me in this and let me rest. If so, I will share my cure with Samuel since he has not fared well since—he has, in fact, descended as on stairs straight into hell, though of course you would forgive him. Well, you did forgive him that very night. Still, he will not recover, and he must. For everyone's sake.

That night. It was a happy eve, we were by the fire, the children all around. Our Rose, our little Emily and Clarence George, wide-eyed babes on the rug staring up at you dancing in your whirling skirts beneath the hanging lamplight. You laughed with Clarence George who tried to dance with you, standing on your feet. You were a sport, my darling girl, a generous light lent us for too short a time. How your mother doted upon you! How we all did! You, of us all, were the brightest prospect for our happy futures. We stood for a time in that *reflected light, as now we languish in the shadows of your absence.*

We pulled taffy. Your mother's sweet tooth ruled the evening! What laughter rang in the parlour. It was as happy an eve as Christmas, all were there. All were lively, and still I see your fair, full cheek bloom, your slender neck and happy, happy features. I must say Rose, then, was taken with some slight jealously, a boy, no doubt, she had fancied, turned his eye to you. But that would not come between you— in the end, our Rose sat with you till you died.

I guess your aching tooth you owed to your mother, since she could not restrain you nor herself from the taffy pulled, and so we retired, but you were pained, and so descended from your bed to find a clove for it, I suppose . . . or so you said. I wonder did you read your last poems as you sat below us, pressing a poultice to your tooth? Those lines, I know, would make your uncle proud had he seen your precocious nature so closely following his. What verse is lost due to the loss of you both!

There, you feel better! Then, to warm yourself a bit before retiring, off to the sofa you went and flounced upon . . . the gun. Your brother's gun. Samuel never will forgive himself. I know this is true. There is nothing in this world will allow him to excuse his error, though an error it was—a mistake. One only is allowed him in this life, and this was it. We lost two children that night, though one still walks this earth.

So the gun discharged into your breast and neck, my darling. My darling! That shot! That I had it in my power to revisit time, to take it back, ah—silly thought. Even to see you once more—our live, vivacious child! The white, fair, rounded face, the happy countenance. That shot! And yet you did not die at once. Your mother, frantic-eyed, flew down the stairs, as did I after her, and the children. There, you weltered in your blood, turned an astonished, horrified eye upon us, though you could not lift yourself, your fair hair so bloodied. A moment before, dancing in your eyes were images of mirth, now they held . . . they barely saw us. Dr. Arthur came, we lifted you up to your bed. He could do nothing.

All night we sat around you, oh how it saddened you—not your own pain—that was no concern to you. You hated what your dying did to us! I saw it in your eyes, heard it in your tearful, welling farewell to your mother. I cannot write this more. I cannot!

Except for Samuel. Except it might heal my dear, brooding boy. Except for that I would not go on.

You lasted the night, and we held you one by one. Samuel was inconsolable, though you held him tenderly, even as your breath drew difficultly. Even then, you whispered your forgiveness. He turned to stone that night, and nevermore has been as he was before. He never will. You passed quietly in the light of morning, as I had just turned to admonish Clarence George to quiet. I turned back, and you'd gone. I've never said goodbye, have I?

I set the entry aside. I thought about how stupid and crass people can be, and all those contemporaneous accounts of Isabelle's suicide; no one who knew this family would draw such a conclusion. I sat there amidst the Seelbach's turn-of-the-century replica breakfront and four-poster bed and felt the family's long ago sorrow as if it were my own.

Exhausted, I stretched out on the lofted bed and fell asleep.

The phone woke me. It was Gray saying they were running late; the meeting would adjourn in half an hour. I was to meet him at the Fitzgerald Suite where Horace and Miriam were staying and where the syndicate meeting was taking place.

Thank God for the call. I'd have slept through the rest of the day and night. I can fall asleep at the drop of a hat and stay that way for a really long time, quite a talent. I was also grateful for the delay since I'm dumber than a doorknob when I wake up. I splashed some water on my face then thought about it and pulled out the soap and gave myself a good scrub. I pulled my hair up and gave it a few twists, securing it in a silver barrette, put on charcoal linen slacks, a white jersey halter, jacket, and took a few swipes with blue eyeliner to help along my eyes and headed to the Fitzgerald Suite right on time. From our dinner conversation the night before, I imagined the morning spent with that big, fat Horace had been a big, fat strain on Gray; Horace seemed way too interested in highlighting Gray's financial difficulties, and I was sure this issue was the main point of the meeting.

Horace was a very distasteful man.

Gray answered the door at my knock; he was dressed in a blue and white striped oxford cloth shirt with dark khakis. He'd rolled the sleeves up to mid-forearm.

He smiled when he saw me and kissed me lightly on the cheek. "How was your day?" he said. "The Filson is worth the trip, isn't it?"

It was, and I said so.

I got only a peek at the suite behind Gray, and had the impression of swag curtains, a 19th century armoire, and a cream colored carpet. Gray shut the door quickly behind him, took my arm, and guided me toward the elevators before I could get a clear view of the rooms.

"How was the meeting?" I said as we hustled along. Where was Gray going in such a damned hurry?

"Good. Good," said Gray, glancing up at the floors clicking down as the elevator descended. We exited at the lobby level. "Come on," he said, "I want to show you something."

I could see that.

We crossed the lobby and headed to the right, then down a curving stairway. Gray and I walked briskly along the hall on the lower level, then into the Rathskeller, a room constructed of Rookwood tiles, said Gray, part of the Seelbach's remodeling in 1907.

"What do you think?" he said as we entered. I could tell he had high hopes for my praise.

Truthfully, it was a dungeon. Reminded me of the 18th century Gothic novels I'd been forced to read as a student. Really dark with heavy Bavarian wood paneling, subtly colored Rookwood tiling, and massive, heavy archways and columns. Lighting so dim it made me feel Nosferatu was hanging out nearby, his scrabbly long fingernails just itching to grab my ankle, crawl up my leg, and sink those long, Dracula teeth deep in my neck.

"Pretty impressive, isn't it?" said Gray gazing around.

Well, yes, it was impressive . . . in a *Cabinet of Dr. Caligari*, horror film sort of way.

"Impressive," I agreed, as we walked further in.

"Pretty much all the important events in my life took place here," said Gray.

Oh my, I thought. I may have seriously misjudged this man's taste.

Gray smiled. "This place was the thorn in my

father's side. "

I could well understand that.

Gray noticed my nod. "No, it's not what you think." He chuckled. "My dad loved this place as much as my mother." He took a long, slow breath and looked around him. "My mother spent a lot of time here, and so did Brett, and my sister. All of us, really. My mother was born and raised in Louisville, and she never really made the transition to Lexington society. Lexington can be pretty intimidating, I guess."

From the amount of money I'd heard routinely spent in and around Lexington—especially at the yearling sales—intimidation made sense. Money often breeds a tungsten-like societal stratification.

"It was tough for my dad to buck that, but my mom felt more at home here," said Gray, looking around and patting a thick, heavy column with odd affection. "I remember coming to visit my Grandpa here, and Brett practically lived here then. When we were kids, we'd race around these columns, and upstairs—we terrorized the place. But," he sighed, "I think they put up with us because of the old man. He was a fixture here, he and his friend Jacoby. The only two men who actually lived here."

Gray was quiet for a time, recalling old memories. I let the time pass without comment.

"My parents were married here. Over there was the bandstand." As we continued through the space, he pointed to the far wall, which now simply depicted a scene from Bavaria at the top and heavy wood paneling below.

"My sister's wedding reception was here, too," he said.

Gray's sister and her husband had moved to Italy five years before; there were wedding pictures on the stairway of Lillian's home visually attesting to Gray's wedding description.

"And my college graduation party was here."

Gray sat down at one of the round, cloth-covered tables. I sat down next to him. Over us ochre-colored Rookwood pelicans stared down from a massive pillar. Clearly, the room held a lot of memories. I sat quietly; it seemed he'd brought me here for a reason.

"I got a call from Tim a while ago," said Gray, without preamble. "We lost another foal."

"Another foal?" A grim heaviness hung in the air between us.

Gray had put his elbows on the table and now slid them back, crossing his arms. "You always lose some," he said, looking at the tablecloth. "At first I didn't think much of it. As I told you, it started early, then by March things were not looking good—the mares were aborting more than usual . . . well, more than usual for us, then it seemed there were a few too many on the ground not making it." He looked at me quietly. "I thought maybe it was the reproductive loss thing come back. Then things got back to normal, but now . . ." He shrugged. "It could just be bad luck."

Of course I immediately thought of Horace. His intensity about "helping" Gray out financially seemed more than coincidence. Perhaps his "help" extended to aiding the failure of Brookfield to further his own gain. I wasn't sure how to bring it up; Gray seemed oblivious to the man's menace.

"And you have no idea what's causing this?" I said.

"Tim's tests still show nothing." He shrugged.

I wasn't sure what to say. "What do you think?"

"I'm not sure what to think," said Gray.

It seemed neither of us wanted to speculate about other causes for the deaths. But Gray had brought me here for a reason. I sensed that part of him suspected something other than natural causes; maybe he needed some

70

prodding.

"Gray," I said quietly, "isn't it possible that someone might intentionally be killing these foals?"

He didn't say anything for a while. He seemed to be brooding a little.

"I know things go on," he said, staring at the tablecloth. "I've been around enough to know that. It's just never touched us." Then he looked at me. "You could kill a horse any number of ways that aren't detectable—calcium, potassium overdose, or insulin . . . Is that what you think is going on?"

It was interesting that he valued my opinion; I knew nothing about his business. My instinct for solving puzzles, for digging up relevant information, putting it together to form a picture that wasn't clear before, made me *feel* more than know that something was very wrong.

"Well, it might be what's going on." I said, carefully. "If you think the number of foals you're losing is out of the ordinary, and if no other farms are having the problem, then yes, I think you have to consider a reason outside of normal ones."

Gray nodded. But he didn't say anything.

"We can't handle much more," he said. "Right now the farm is holding on by a thread."

I wasn't aware his financial difficulties were that strained. It lent support to the idea that someone might want to take advantage of him, move in for the kill . . . perhaps all too literally. "Who knows about how difficult things are?"

Gray looked at me. We both knew what I was thinking, the name just needed to be said out loud.

Gray looked over toward the little fretted wood balcony just to our left. "Right under there was where my sister and her husband cut the cake. I can see it as clearly as if it happened yesterday." He seemed even more subdued.

"And right there sat Horace and Miriam, Brett and Grandpa, all the employees, even a few friends from Japan came over—we all sat together. Everyone was here celebrating."

I had wanted to talk to Gray about Brett. "You said Brett was here?"

"Oh, yeah, like I said, he practically lived here. Grandpa hardly ever left the place, in fact. He and that buddy of his, Jacoby, both lived here from 1905 on. From when the hotel was built. Jacoby, as I recall, moved out in 1950 to a rest home, but Grandpa was here until the day he died."

I tried to broach my concerns about Brett gently. "Gray, I know he's your cousin, but you and Brett, I don't know . . . you don't seem very close, I guess. It seemed you spent time together when you were young . . . what happened?"

Gray thought it over. "Well, I don't think anything really *happened*. He was pretty much always with Grandpa, and I guess I only saw him when mother and I came over here. Then I went off to school and Brett tried the jockey thing. I don't know, I guess we just never had a lot in common after Grandpa passed."

That made sense I supposed. Still, Brett lived practically in Gray's lap, and I wondered what he thought of him as an adult so I asked.

"He's as capable as they come." Gray replied to my question. I could tell he didn't know where I was going with these questions.

"He's spoken to you about his little box?"

Gray laughed. "Oh, yes. He thinks there's millions hid somewhere. It's his Keats mania. Did he talk to you, too?" Gray's tone held an ever-so-slight sharpness to it.

"Not really. He just seemed nervous, and I wondered why."

"Huh," said Gray. "Can't imagine." Then he lapsed into silence again. I supposed it had to do with the mention of money. Gray seemed as reluctant to talk about his family as was his mother. He shook his head. "So you really think someone could be purposefully hurting my foals?" He was also adept at changing the subject.

I didn't press him. I considered the tone of his question and could tell he'd prefer if I answered in the negative, told him my feelings about purposeful harm coming to more and more of his foals was simply a dark illusion born of this dark, foreboding room.

I couldn't say that. "I think you have to consider it."

"Who would do that?" He seemed genuinely at a loss.

"Who would benefit?"

Again the name hung in the air between us.

"Julia, I've known Horace my whole life. His family and mine have been connected forever. There is no reason why he would want to see me fail. He'd go under, too."

"Not if he owned the major share in Brookfield *and* the stallions, *and* his broodmares, *and* his runners," I said. I'd learned a little something over the past few months. "Isn't that what the meeting was about this morning?"

Gray hesitated. "Partly."

He swiveled in his seat to face me. "But it doesn't make sense. My family and Miriam's and Horace's have been like one family for as long as I can remember." He looked around the room, likely I thought, calling up ghosts of parties past.

"Miriam's father sat right over there at my ninth birthday party," he said, pointing to the bar area. "Close to the bourbon, that was Shorty all right." He seemed thoughtful. "He was a talented trainer. Knew bloodlines like nobody I've ever seen. Knew how to get the most out of horses." Gray stopped. "Shorty was one of the main reasons

Brookfield succeeded."

"One of the reasons?" I said.

"That's just it," said Gray, forcefully. "It's taken all of us. All of us working together over the years. Not just Shorty. Not just Horace, or me. All of us. That's why it doesn't make sense that Horace would do something like that." Gray shook his head. Then he looked back at the bar area.

"It broke my father's heart when Shorty went down. It broke his heart." Gray looked at me. "Can you understand that?"

Obviously the prospect of Horace having anything to do with sabotaging Brookfield was inconceivable to Gray. I did understand what he was telling me. I also understood that the allure of money sometimes outweighed the ties of family.

"Of course," I said.

"Horace is harmless. He talks a lot, but his heart is in the right place."

I wondered. "What happened with your father and Shorty?" I asked, trying to move Gray away from the subject of Horace. I'd already made up my mind to do a little research on my own.

"Drinking is a big problem in the industry. Always has been. And drugs, too. People say they want to deal with it, but really they don't," said Gray. "You have your needle horses on the track, but you've got the same problem off the track. Shorty was one of the best, but he just couldn't stay away from the booze or the drugs. He'd hit a horse up with heroin, and then himself. This was way back, before all the testing. My father was not into drugs and put a stop to it. It got so he couldn't deal with Shorty." Gray paused.

"Heroin?" I said. "No kidding."

"Oh, yeah. They run like hell on it. Trainers will zap a horse with electrodes—they call them machine horses, even now you'll see that, milk-shake them. Now I hear there's stuff to increase red blood cells—really it doesn't end. Just like with other athletes, trainers are always after an edge." Gray looked up at the fretted balcony. "There's a lot of pressure in the game," he said. "A lot."

It didn't surprise me.

"Anyway," continued Gray, "after so many years, and Shorty getting worse and worse, my father had to let him go. There wasn't anything else to do—Shorty wouldn't admit he had a problem. Can't cure it if you don't have it." Gray smiled. "He was a great guy. Told the raunchiest jokes I ever heard, before or since; what I learned about sex from him went way beyond the breeding shed." He chuckled. "He really was something."

"So what happened to him?" I said.

Gray turned somber. "What happens to a lot of them. Jockeys especially. Especially back then. He just went down after he left us. Just down and out. Somewhere in Mexico. I never did really hear. Don't think Miriam knows either."

Gray looked around the Rathskeller, squinting into its darkened recesses. "I don't think anyone really wanted to know."

7

When I got home, the first thing I did was fire up the computer. I wasn't Gwyneth's best friend for nothing; she'd taught me a little about financial B&E. I felt an insistence about proving to Gray that Horace was in a position to do him harm. I wanted to look at Horace's finances; I had a bad feeling about the guy and I wanted to know if he was connected to Gray's increasing problems.

But I was a novice, and that was clear in short order. I couldn't get past even the most rudimentary blocks to the Laroveneurs' finances. I'd have to give it up or call Gwyneth.

She arrived at my place quickly, though I'd had to explain why I needed her help (leaving out the Keats issue) to get her to come. Gwyneth enjoys pitting her wits against other computer geeks, especially in the service to a good cause. She'd met Gray at the sale, and considered him worth the effort.

She spent a requisite few minutes communing with Albert—they have chemistry and can't tolerate long absences from each other—and then she got down to business, Albert plopping down with a contented moan at her feet.

"Do you know his social security number?" she said.

Of course I didn't know Horace's social security number.

"Where does he bank?" she said.

I didn't know that, either.

Gwyneth scowled at me, and I have to say, there was a measure of condescension in her manner. "How can I help you if I don't have even the smallest bit of information?"

I gave her the syndicate name. That appeased her. In a brief time she'd gone from window to window, clicking away on the keyboard and clucking like a satisfied little hen.

"Hmmm," she said after a time and turned to me. "Can't be Horace. He's nearly broke. It's the wife with all the money—and the broodmares. It looks like the horses they race . . . that's odd," Gwyneth said and paused. "For some reason all their assets are held separately."

Gwyneth scratched Albert's head absently as she enlarged the screen showing Horace's financial statement. I peered over her shoulder then sat back and listened. "The only thing it looks like Horace owns outright is his stake in a horse called Aurora's Prospect. And a few other stallions. But his most significant holding is that one horse."

Aury. The stallion Gray said was poised to make a great leap forward in stud fees.

Horace's actions though, overall, were odd, I thought. If he was almost broke why had he been putting so much pressure on Gray to sell to him?

"What about the syndicate?" I said.

Gwyneth closed some windows and studied the screen. "The syndicate is all right. There's money in there, but if I was a member of that syndicate, and I knew about Horace, he'd be gone. There's likely a clause in there for these situations." She studied the screen again. "Actually

Horace doesn't have a large participation here. Looks like he's sold off some of his interest to others in the syndicate over the last few years." She looked up. "Maybe they do know and are just squeezing him out."

So how was Horace planning to buy out Gray? Use his wife's money? Seemed to me if their money was separated there was a reason for that; it seemed unlikely Miriam would be financing him, in that case. I knew Horace must have some money; he had a foal out of Aury every year, which he'd probably been selling and his other, smaller syndicate participation . . . plus a cut from the stud fees, which given those figures, would have returned him some money. How could he possibly be broke?

"Gambling?" suggested Gwyneth.

I thought about the billboards strewn across the Kentucky landscape: *Gambling May Be An Addiction*, they read.

"Maybe," I said. "You could be right."

After Gwyneth printed out all the financial information for me and left, I pulled out George's journal. I began at the first entry of the journal once again. I'd been working my way through it in chronological order and in the process had gained a growing, insistent sympathy for George Keats. Seeing how slightly built he was in the Filson portrait made me realize how difficult life in the wilderness must have been for him. This, coupled with John J. Audubon's crass observation about the inadequacy of his wood-chopping ability and yet George's undaunted persistence, gave me a respect for the man who'd come here feeling burdened to support his wife and the two brothers and sister he'd left back in England. George worked very hard and had a love of and flair for writing poetry, though he would eternally be regarded as inferior to his illustrious brother. He'd raised a large family yet was also an active and responsible citizen.

78

It seemed out of keeping that such a man could ever be the financial drain on his brother he was described to be or that he would lie. The reports at his passing indicating he was bankrupt were at odds with what he, himself, stated in his journal. There could only be one conclusion. The reports were wrong. George had provided for his family, but where had the money gone?

I opened the black journal to George's last entries, the ones he'd made in the knowledge he was dying.

> *August 21, 1841*
>
> *I am feverish, and the heat exhausts me. I wish not to send for the doctor for it would alarm Georgiana.*

> *August 28, 1843*
>
> *A week and I cannot yet stir from bed.*

> *September 2, 1841*
>
> *This day, I am somewhat revived following a prolonged enervation.*
>
> *I must, therefore, write all that I am able this day. I will begin, but whether I last to its ending is a question I cannot answer.*
>
> *I met again last eve with Samuel and my fears grow as my strength diminishes. He is so like his mother, a sweet boy with strength he does not know he owns. I must make a man of Samuel, he is of the age. What is to come is a man's task, and he must see to the care of the rest.*
>
> *Yet the boy cowers. I fear I must prevail upon him again and perhaps again, and I have little time left.*

There was a period of a month, and then the entries

resume, but with a much darker tone.

November 15, 1841

Much occupies me. The fever comes and goes, and my chest is tight, the blood comes more often. I feel more piercingly than ever before how terrible was my own absence from John as he lingered on this very path. This dying is hellish.

The house is still. Yet not still, since all of you—my dear children, my grieving Georgiana—populate it even though gone for a time, gaily, as you, one by one, came in to wish me well before your outing to the Granger's small party. I have just stoked the fire, I have not breath to bring it to a full blaze, but how my little venture exhausts me! To content myself, I picture your small fingers, Alice Ann, in your mother's sturdy palm, and by your side our serious Ella, marching, pulling at her bonnet as she goes. You leave a bit behind, here with me, all of you, which I sense lying here by the fire. I rest in this. I know when my time comes—and it draws so close I can see, at times, the end—you will be around me, you will comfort me in our family's practiced art.

But then, dying is a solitary act. No one joins you, no one follows.

George had a little over a month to live when he wrote this; I pictured him lying in his bed in the upper floors of his beloved gray stone Louisville mansion. He'd left Red Banks and Audubon after his financial disaster and started over in Louisville. With his years of philanthropic, literary, and commercial work, his home had become the center of arts and culture in the city. He and Georgiana had hosted parties, art lectures, and dinners with the city's luminaries and politicians. With his death only a month off, this entry seemed to me an anguished one, especially in his concern for Samuel.

How hard it must have been for George to see Samuel's unending decline. It seemed that George's retelling of Isabelle's death hadn't exorcized the old ghosts after all. Twice George voices concern for Samuel's strength. It must have panicked him to think of leaving his wife and large family to the care of an eldest son incapable of the task.

Yet, knowing Samuel's handicap, George nonetheless did assign him the task most crucial to the family's survival

A few pages on George had written:

December 3, 1841
> *The blood comes—a bright, awful color— and I think continually of my dear brother John, and Tom, and Mother who have passed this way. What unlikely luck.*

> *I don't have strength to write all that is in my mind. So Samuel, I'll set down here what I shall tell you before I die. You must heed me. I shall put this book away against an untimely loss.*

> *They think I die penniless. Yet I have secured much wealth. I am not a fool. I have put much aside, bit by bit, and have done so since John's passing, aware his fate might someday fall to me. As it has.*

> *No one shall touch it, no hand shall take this rich treasure from you—I have secured it and only you, Samuel, shall search it out. My hope rests in you.*

> *How it exhausts me to write this. John, Tom, Mother . . . and Isabelle. I will see soon*

enough.

George had only a few weeks to live when he wrote this. The mention of blood occurs in the letters of John Keats, as well—this is why George comments on the family's "unlikely luck," I guessed; of the immediate family, only his father and sister Fanny escaped the consumptive's death. I felt his terrible sadness at having to further burden Samuel. Maybe that's why George put away his journal, as insurance against Samuel not being up to the task George set him. It must have been really tough for the young Samuel to watch his mother marry a year after his father's death. Even if Samuel was somehow able to follow his father's instructions, I thought, it seemed logical he'd do everything in his power to see that his father's money didn't to go to his new step-father. The last point made me feel sure the money hadn't left George's hiding place during Samuel's care of it.

But how much was there, and where was it?

I also wondered why, if George was so aware of Samuel's problems, he would insist on giving him the responsibility for the family treasure. Why not tell Georgiana, or John Henry, who was only a year or so younger than Samuel? I recalled that women in the mid-19th century were still viewed as having "weak minds"; fifty years or so before George's death, Mary Wollstonecraft had railed against women valued as fainting beauties and nothing more. George was a gallant man but a man of his era nonetheless. Caring for the family would fall to the eldest son and to no one else.

I thought about how, in another entry, George had stressed the importance of caring for "the urn."

My mind leapt to John's "Ode on a Grecian Urn." Of course when George died, John was a recognized poet in England, but could George have realized the value of John's original copy? It seemed unlikely. Still, John had thought this ode was his best. And George himself was a poet, a talented one, some say. In fact, scholars have noted that though a lot of the poems are signed with John's initials, there are some marked "GK," and some without any marking at all. Perhaps George had possessed such uncanny foresight. Maybe he'd even written the ode himself.

In the end, I doubted this was the case. Especially because there was another more plausible possibility; maybe the "urn" was a real urn. I pictured a big silver urn somewhere overflowing with jewels and gold coins. The image wasn't all that far-fetched; lots of people had buried valuables during the early wars in this country. Gray said the silver Preakness Cup had been buried at Woodburn during the Civil War so it wouldn't be taken in a pillaging raid. Perhaps George had buried his treasure to avoid the bankruptcy pillage.

The final entry in George's journal was simple:

December 23, 1841

I think of what you'll do, my family, going into your lives without my observations. Samuel, I leave these last entries for you. As you read this, know that as the Eldest, you have responsibilities. Dying is a hard thing, but truly I think living, for you, must be the harder task. I acknowledge this, Samuel. But the grief you feel, your own life's prospects dying—no good will come of it. I tell you truthfully, you dishonor Isabelle. She lives in God now, her sweet disposition a happiness to her Eternal Father who keeps her safe and eternally fair. Trust her to His care, Samuel. You are a man, now, and must turn to the living. Care for those I entrust to you.

George had died the following day, on Christmas Eve. What a sad holiday, I thought. While the rest of Louisville was having Christmas pudding and opening presents, the Keats family was preparing to bury their father.

Brett had mentioned clues that he couldn't understand in our conversation about what was in his box. It was true, I didn't know where George's money was. I didn't know where his brother's ode was. But I had come to know where George Keats' heart was—how unsettled it was at his death and how he wanted nothing more than to care for his family.

I may not have known the whereabouts of Keats' treasure, but I did know where to find Brett.

8

However, before I could meet with Brett, the curator of European visual arts told me to fetch Lillian's written permission to send off the "sketch" to the New York Historical Society. That's where Audubon's original paintings are housed and where various electronic, possibly chemical, and certainly more narrowly focused expertise could be used to authenticate the painting.

It appears the "sketch" might be quite the find, Alex told me, slightly disgruntled that his own opinion wasn't enough for his boss. Evidently Audubon had a perfectionist streak, a trait I obviously admire, in that he often made "sketches" like Lillian's before the hand-colored etchings he's so famous for. This one was unusual because Audubon only made two painting of swans, and both were of single white swans. Lillian's were Trumpeter Swans—in the plural—and one was black, the only black swan Audubon ever painted. There seemed quite a stir brewing in the ornithological art world.

Though I could have asked Lillian to fax her permission, instead I made a quick call to Gray to ascertain Brett's schedule and to see if Lillian was available for said "official" permission-granting. I can be inventive when I need to.

Brett, said Gray, got to work at 6:30 in the morning and usually got off around four or five, if nothing went wrong. He often had to go back at six-thirty or seven at night to help turn out the stallions. Though I knew *where* to find him, I wasn't quite sure how best to catch him.

"Just come down. I'll call mother, and you can talk to Brett when you get here. We'll arrange something. Just come. I'll have the guest cottage ready in about an hour," said Gray in answer to my request for help.

I hadn't thought about actually staying at Brookfield; I'd considered just a quick trip down and back, but a stay sounded inviting. After my classes that day, I wasn't due to teach again until the following Tuesday, and I was caught up at the library, so I'd have most of five days if I left right after classes that afternoon. It would give me plenty of time to talk to Brett and compare Keats' journal with my collection of Keats correspondence. Plus, I'd have some time to spend with Lillian.

Funny how suddenly the urgency of getting Lillian's permission back to the university faded in view of a possible five-day hiatus. Oh well, the "sketch" had been rolled up for who knows how long; I trusted it could stay that way another couple of days. Or, of course, I could use Gray's office fax.

Problem solved.

I told Gray I'd be there around two or two-thirty, asked him to mention my visit to Brett, and packed up all my research materials. After a quick call to Gwyneth, I dropped Albert off at her house, watched him bound into her very large yard, then headed down Interstate 75.

I arrived at the farm a bit before two o'clock. The guest cottage was a late-1800s rough-cut limestone house just up the hill from the office. The door was unlocked so I unloaded my knapsack, hauled in my laptop, books, and backpack filled with notes and papers, and hefted everything onto the mahogany table just inside the door.

The place was clean and comfortable, and had the rustic feel of a cabin. I felt as if I should make a fire below the carved wood mantle, but it was sixty-five degrees outside so I restrained myself. The kitchen, living area, and dining table were in one big room. To the right was a short hallway with a bathroom on the left and a bedroom on the right with a queen-sized bed that included an ornately carved oak headboard. The living room had an overstuffed couch that folded out into a queen-size bed, a TV with satellite connection, and a coffee table covered with stallion brochures from nearby farms. The place was cool and quiet.

A red truck drove by; then another truck with a horse trailer attached; then a big yellow machine that looked like an iron insect with a load of hay on the back whizzed by. Then it was quiet again.

Ten to two. I threw my knapsack on the bed, left my backpack on the table, and headed out onto the porch for a moment before heading down the hill to the stallion complex where I thought I'd find Gray.

Two mares grazed in the paddock to the left of the cottage, and I walked over to the fence, leaning on the topmost rail. One was a copper chestnut, the other a deep bay. I watched them for minutes, not moving, but I could have stayed for hours. The chestnut stepped forward once, precisely, one foreleg in place just ahead of the other, so that the great curve of her neck slowly lowered her head to the new grass, the mane shifting slightly. In a slow ballet, their soft muzzles drifted over the grass, the shoulder shifted, then another step, pause, graze, shift, step, pause, graze . . . . I knew they were products, manufactured almost, and bred consciously towards profit. But what I looked at defied that, exceeding those ends by what they'd become. Standing there, two graceful, sculpted creatures whose perfection existed incidental to me, they grazed oblivious that their beauty defeated the industry built around them. Serenely themselves, at home in their grace, they lived in a sort of timelessness I could never achieve, grazing in the mid-day sun, shimmering copper and deep bay, simply and endlessly being.

A truck with an attached horse trailer pulled up outside the breeding shed down the hill, startling the mares. By the time their heads rose from the grasses, they'd already taken flight, their bodies still as the surface of a lake, while beneath them, legs gathered in the paddock spaces effortlessly, heads and necks forward, flat backed, tails high and streaming, they skimmed the flat surfaces to the curving fence line, their bodies at rest in motion. They didn't seem to touch the earth.

God they were beautiful. It didn't matter how much trouble they were. Beauty, I thought, can be as addicting as winning.

Below, at the stallion barn, a mare was backed out of the trailer, and I heard the stallions start their high, tense whinnies that descended the scale, ending in a low, menacing rumble.

I watched the mare being led into the breeding shed and caught a glimpse of Gray poking his head out of the stallion barn; he looked up my way and waved.

Tim Bradford was just getting out of his truck, and we all met at the corner of the barn.

"Hey, Julia," said Tim. "Come to see the new guy?"

Gray motioned me to stand to the right at the other edge of the doorway. "Let Richard get him out, and then you come stand over there," said Gray, pointing to the stall just inside the doorway. "Tim's checking Devil's Dream."

"Need to see what we've got," said Tim. "If he'll breed."

He motioned so that Richard brought Devil around

88

to stand with his flank and shoulder up against the wall. The stallion seemed to grow bigger the closer he came to me; his bay coat glowed even in the light of the barn. He raised his head and turned a suspicious eye to me, the whites showing a bit. There was some tension in the air.

"Whoa, boy," murmured Richard and gave a little on the lead. Devil pranced a moment, then seemed to conclude it was all right for me to be there, so he stepped to the wall. Richard gathered the shank into his hand and held him close.

"Tim's measuring him for insurance," said Gray, "and then Fantasia over there," Gray indicated the mare I'd seen stepping out of the trailer, "will help us check his libido." He grinned at Tim and Richard.

Brett walked in, nodded to me, and passed out onto the gravel. Behind him came my least favorite groom—the one who'd not wanted to give Circuit Breaker the time of day; Chaney followed Brett out, then circled back to the other side of the barn.

Tim rolled over a table with a monitor on it, stood right beside Devil's near back leg and reached under him. Devil tried to sidestep, but he was against the wall. Next he tried to turn, but Richard had hold of him and was so calm up by his head that Devil settled and let Tim grab and measure parts of him I doubt he'd had handled in quite that way before.

"What's the matter with him?" I asked Gray.

He looked fit and healthy and to be truthful, a little scary to me.

"He's fine. Bowed a tendon, and they couldn't bring him back, so he's been sent to stud. He's our new stallion, off the track in California. We've had him here . . . how long now, Richard?"

Richard didn't take his eyes off Devil. "Some weeks."

Gray said, "We just wanted him settled in a bit, now

we'll see how he'll do at his new job."

Marcy, the office manager, walked in. Having been around horses all her life, she positioned herself next to me, well out of Devil's striking distance, and stood quietly with her arms crossed until Tim was done. He noted a few things on the monitor screen and made some notations on his papers and wheeled the contraption out to the gravel.

"Let's see how he likes the ladies," he said, as I looked over his shoulder to see a mare being led placidly toward the other doorway by Brett.

Devil caught the mare's scent and began snorting and pawing, then reared, calling intensely in a wail that rose feverishly, and then fell low in his throat to an ominous growl. It wasn't a question, as in *How about a dance, honey?* but a prelude to savagery . . . or that's what it sounded like to me. Fantasia's eyes widened and she stepped gingerly, attempting to pull away from Brett.

Devil yanked Richard's arm, then the stallion bounced backwards, angling his head sideways. He was very powerful and Marcy put an arm across me, backing us both away quickly.

"Hey, boy," said Richard, following Devil, looking up into his face and letting him have his head.

One scary hunk of horseflesh.

Devil roared and was now physically excited; he'd backed up enough to catch a glimpse of the mare to his right, and Richard's soft calmness had no effect on him.

He pawed and snorted, a serious bundle of hormones dancing in an ancient ritual. Richard stayed right with him. Gray had moved to the stallion's off side, but out of striking range.

Gray was smiling.

Marcy looked at me and whispered, "Poor guy doesn't get it. On the track every time that thing dropped out it'd get snapped with a towel."

I inched nonchalantly to my right, trying to get behind Marcy as we maneuvered to get a look at the mare's back end and Devil in his confused, but ready-for-action state. Chaney held the mare's head still, her lip twitched, and Brett had wrapped her near front leg in a leather strap so she wouldn't kick Devil in his multi-million-dollar parts.

The other stallions who'd raised the call as Fantasia was led in had settled down, perhaps understanding that this wasn't their turn after all.

Now Devil's neck arched, his tail flared, and he pranced toward the mare. It seemed to me he wasn't altogether sure of what to do once he got there; he bobbed his head, prancing sideways.

The mare turned her twitched lip at him. Chaney wrenched the twitch, unnecessarily, I thought, and the mare stiffened but stood still.

Now Devil bounced alongside the mare, and in one sudden move, he turned, hauling Richard around with him, and heaved himself up onto the mare's back with his two front legs. The problem was he was facing us; his rear was at the mare's head.

"Devil, you are one confused boy," said Marcy, laughing. Gray's eyes twinkled.

Only Richard seemed forced to concentrate.

After letting Devil rest on her back for a second, the mare side-stepped and threw him off.

Offended, the young stallion bucked, then finding himself at right angles to the mare's flank, humped and gave her a sharp thwack with both hind legs sending her sideways momentarily before she, too, tried to take aim.

Quickly she and Devil were separated.

"Poor guy," said Marcy.

"Poor guy?" I said. The mare's the one got kicked.

Gray came over after they'd settled Devil and put him back in his stall.

"Well, that was the idea." He seemed pleased.

Marcy headed back to the office and Chaney to parts unknown. Brett led the mare outside, out of pheromone-range, and looked pointedly over at me.

"Excuse me," I said to Gray and walked over to Brett in the sunlight. He nodded and headed for the stallion office to confer with Tim.

"Gray said you come to see me," Brett said as I reached him. He gave me a long, questioning look as if trying to determine my intentions. He stroked the mare's neck absentmindedly.

"I did."

"Well, I'm getting off around four, and then I got to be back at six for the night shift over to the foaling barn. Will you come at a bit after four? I just live over that rise in a little house they give me." He seemed to have arrived at a decision, a slight relief showing in his shoulder set as he stroked the mare's neck and gathered up her lead.

"Yes, that would be fine," I said. "I did want to look at your box, if that would be a good time."

Brett looked pleased. "Yeah. I'd be glad for ye to do it then."

9

I wandered around the farm after leaving Brett, mulling over recent events and the dark mist I continued to feel but couldn't quite penetrate. The tensions, the mysteries, the deaths . . . everything lay just below the surface, murky and ill-defined. I felt frustrated and confused—two emotions my logical, orderly self can't tolerate for long.

Having meandered over the bridge, past the mares pasture, and up over the rise, I soon found myself at Lillian's garden gate. She was cutting lilacs and upon seeing me, invited me in for blueberry scones and coffee.

To be truthful, I suddenly felt overwhelmed and it happened quite unexpectedly somewhere between the barn and Lillian's garden. In addition to the vague but palpable tensions I felt, the past and the present seemed on a collision course I couldn't fathom—Keats in London. Keats in Kentucky. Audubon. Brett and his Grandfather. Lillian. Gray and the Seelbach's Rathskellar. Horace. Miriam. The shuddering financial straits of Brookfield.

How were the past and the present connected? I felt confounded by the number of questions I had and the total lack of answers.

"Julia, are you feeling well?" Lillian said sweetly, motioning me to sit and staring at me through narrowed brows.

I sank into the floral chintz across from her. "I'm well," I said, "and I'm confused."

"Oh, I see," she said, sitting quite still.

I dug up from the depths of myself a straightforward question. "Lillian," I began, "what the hell is going on around here?"

She blinked at me. "Going on?" she repeated.

I glanced around the room. Peach and yellows abounded. Bright cheeriness everywhere—in the curtains, in the smoothly groomed rug, in the tasseled throw pillows, the lampshades. All this cheeriness amid all these dark undercurrents.

"Yes, Lillian," I said, "what, I repeat, is going on?"

And oddly, she smiled.

"Ah, I see," she said, and rested her arm on the nearby down-filled, peach-colored pillow. "You mean about the family."

"Yes, that's exactly what I mean. The family, the farm . . . ."

We sat in silence I refused to break, and then finally she spoke.

"Let's have a bourbon, shall we?" She rose, went to the breakfront, took out two tiny fluted glasses with beaded-glass at the base, and poured two dark brown shots.

"My mother's," she said, handing me a glass. "Odd and strangely attractive, aren't they?"

Yes, but we were not going to chitchat.

She settled back across from me. I sipped my bourbon.

She began to talk, and I didn't interrupt.

"Gray's father was a fierce man. You had to be in those days. Fierce, but that man would do anything to save

94

a horse . . . Unlike," she said more quietly, "some others. Then, and now."

Yes, I had read up on the number of horses euthanized on the tracks.

I sat quietly and I sipped.

"I loved that man," Lillian confided. "And he loved this farm. These horses." She looked at me. "Don't let Gray fool you. This is a business to some. But not to Gray's father and not to Gray."

Well, that was news. Gray had certainly acted as if it was business.

She continued. "These horses get in you. They get inside you, and you are unable to get rid of it. It's a sort of sickness, and Gray is sick nearly to death. It's something that was in Gray's father, and it's in him."

I'd seen that in Gray, that fierce insistence to make a go of Brookfield, now that Lillian mentioned it. I just attributed it more to pride or responsibility than to love.

"Now, he'll say differently, I know. This mess we're in has nearly taken everything out of him."

She paused. "You know there was a time his father and I tried to get him away from all this. We sent him east. We encouraged him to leave this life behind. It was his father, really; he saw that these horses might someday eat that boy alive."

I was quiet, not knowing quite what to say. It wasn't at all how I'd pictured Gray.

She softened. "Oh, now. Perhaps it's wrong to put it like that. Gray's heart is here on this land with these horses. That's always been true, and I suppose it's not a bad thing to follow your heart."

She looked at me expectantly.

I wasn't sure how to respond. Her words, and then that knowing look she cast my way, caught me off guard. Her last comment touched something in me, I realized, something I wasn't at all prepared to deal with just now.

As she continued to gaze at me quietly, I felt my face flush. Yes, ok, I had to admit I found Gray an attractive man. A good man, as far as I could tell. And if I was being honest with myself, I was developing feelings for him. Feelings I couldn't trust at the moment. Events at the farm had left me with a sense of foreboding, as if something dark was at work just out of sight. I'd be a fool to give in to my emotions, I thought. Gray might well be involved in sinister acts.

I wouldn't let myself. Not until I was sure, very sure, that Gray was the man his mother raised him to be.

Lillian smiled at me. Suddenly I felt very uncomfortable. Were my feelings for Gray so close to the surface even she could see them?

"It's not a bad thing to follow your heart, Julia," she said again, softly.

Her words made me feel exposed as well as embarrassed. Lillian seemed to see straight through me. I left abruptly, her words weighing heavily on my heart and mind.

10

He answered the door in his blue jeans, and that was it—no shirt, no shoes.

"Hey," said Brett as he opened the screen door, looking as if he'd just gotten out of bed. It was four-thirty, and I'd walked around after leaving Lillian's, uncomfortable and more than a bit embarrassed.

I'd gotten her signature on the curator's permission form and left her house quickly, making my way back over the rise and heading for the privacy of the guesthouse to wait out the time until I was due at Brett's.

Seeing his sleepy, somewhat overly casual form in the doorway, I wondered if Brett was just catching up on a few winks before heading back to work. "Come on in. And 'scuse me, I'll just put on a shirt."

He disappeared for a minute, then reappeared with his darkened cigar box and set it down on the oak table in the kitchen. He pulled the window shade and turned on the light, motioning for me to sit.

"Now mind you," he said, "I can't really say what's here. I just have that feeling, ye know?"

His yellow hair stuck out in dry clumps, and he tried to smooth it back behind both ears. Unsuccessfully.

"I understand," I said, feeling my discomfort fade as I slid into the chair and prepared to look over the Keats artifacts.

"It's just that my daddy and my grand-pa did not speak for years. Did not get along et-al. Then my daddy died." He sat down across from me, the box between us. "My grand-pa and I, we always got along. So I have special interest in understanding what all is in this box."

Now that I had a moment to see it more closely, I realized the box was very old but not an antique; rather it was a fairly ubiquitous dirty and faded Cuban cigar box. Brett flipped up the top, and I stared at the contents.

"There's that splinter, and I don't know what it's wrapped in." He picked up a long piece of wood—it really was a splinter—wrapped in extremely old, yellowed, and brittle lace.

He laid it carefully to the side of the box on the table.

"Then this drawing or sketch or something," he said, picking out a single sheet of thick, browned paper on which was drawn what looked like an architectural sketch of a post or a support for a wall or, as Brett had said originally, a pillar of some sort. This he placed next to the piece of wood.

"This is what I told you about, the writing I can't figure."

Brett handed me a scrap of paper which was in fact signed *Samuel Keats*. On it, in a scrolled hand and in fading black ink, it said: *The secret is safe with Isabelle.*

The words echoed in my thought. *Isabelle.* George's journal entries came back to me, and I saw he had been correct; Isabelle's death did seem to haunt Samuel. Did this scrap comment relate to Samuel's secret—that it was his gun that had killed his sister—or to George's? I wasn't sure; I did know that whatever the answer, it had something to

98

do with Isabelle and perhaps her death.

Brett carefully took the scrap from my hand and laid it next to the other two items on the table.

"Now here's an odd bird," he said. He looked up at me, out from under his prominent brows, and smiled. He'd made a joke. "Ye see this postcard?" he said. "It's a bird, a pelican, from Florida, an it's from my grand-pa to his friend Jacoby over to the Seelbach when they both lived there." He held out the postcard for me to see.

I flipped it over and read: "Having a wonderful time. This is the most beautiful place. And so quiet, with sweet drinks, happy people, and fair weather. Truly beautiful—what else do we need?   Your faithful friend."

I had a nagging feeling . . . something was familiar about what Brett's grandfather had written, but I couldn't quite grasp it. I sat there quietly, staring at the postcard. I flipped it over and looked at the picture. Just a plain, brown Florida pelican sitting on a pier post, nothing special. I turned it to the text side and read the words again, quietly to myself. I glanced up at Brett who sat there patiently. What was it that bothered me? I wondered.

Suddenly I saw it, or maybe heard it in my own murmurings. *sweet, happy, fair* . . . an odd combination of words to occur both on the postcard in front of me and in the journal less than a quarter-mile away, in my backpack lying on the mahogany coffee table in the guest cottage. Not much to go on, really, but I felt something significant had just happened though I had no idea what it was. I looked up at Brett and felt a physical thrill not unlike what I'd seen in Devil that afternoon. But this was not sexual, and unlike the stallion, I knew exactly what to do. Follow the clues, piece together the puzzle, and . . . .

"Brett, do you think this postcard and the scrap were both written by your grandfather?" I said.

He handed me the scrap of paper signed by Samuel

Keats. I compared it to the Florida postcard. They were definitely written by two different people.

"Naw. That scrap is by my Great-grand-pa, like I told ye. Sam Keats."

"Sam Keats," I said.

"Yeah, and then there's all this rubble." Brett got up and tore a paper towel off the roll on the kitchen counter, folded it and laid it beside the other contents on the table. Then he poured out a small mound of bluish dust and, as he said, rubble.

"What is that?" I said.

Brett stared at it. "Durned if I know."

We both sat in silence staring at the artifacts.

After a few moments Brett scooted back his chair and put one ankle over the other knee. "So do you think there's something here?"

He jiggled his foot. "Or am I nuts?"

I liked Brett. He had an intuition, and even though he didn't understand why he had it, he was willing to make a fool of himself to find out if it were true or not.

"No, I don't think you're crazy," I said. "But let me ask you something."

"You go right ahead."

I thought about how to phrase this. "You said you had a feeling."

"Yeah."

"You think these are clues to something?"

He nodded. "I do."

"Is there anything else that would suggest that? Or can you think of what they might be clues to?"

Brett was quiet for a moment. "Ye mean besides it bein' in the bank box?"

"Yes, besides that."

"Well, I'll tell ye the truth. Ye see my grand-pa he never worked. He just lived over to the Seelbach, and my

100

daddy and everybody thought poorly of him, and he never said how he come by his money. There are others say that he give Gray's daddy money, too, but then again, where was the money? So there was some speculation about all that."

Brett stopped and got up to get a coke. "You want anything? I got juice or Mountain Dew, if you like."

"Coke," I said.

He got a glass of ice for me and a coke, then sat down with his can and resumed.

"So you probably know, being a teacher and knowing about Keats, that my grand-pa's grand-pa—that would be George Keats—they said the same thing about him. That he was a penniless guy, and he sucked out the money from his famous brother in England."

I nodded.

"Well, that don't sit well with me."

I nodded again.

Brett scratched his blue jeans over his knee. "I knowed my grand-pa. He wasn't like that. And I suspect neither was his grand-pa. So there's that feeling, too."

"How do you think your grandfather got his money, then?" I said. I poured the coke and drank a sip. It was cold, fizzy, and I was suddenly very thirsty.

"Well, there was a lot of gambling over there at that time," he said, "though my grand-pa was not the gambling sort. Al Capone was there; I suppose you know. But I guess that could have been it. Or . . . "

"You think he had another source of income?"

Brett studied his can, squeezed it slightly. "I don't know. I just have this odd feeling."

He stared at the artifacts, then up at me. "Ye know what I mean?"

I did.

That evening Gray and I had an early dinner at a

small restaurant with plastic covering the chair seats, and a TV turned to the sports channel in the dining room.

"Sorry, I have to have a quick dinner and turn in early," said Gray, in apology for the atmosphere. "Big day tomorrow." He'd had on a khaki Brookfield Stud ball cap when he'd picked me up, and now he set it on the table and ran a hand through his hair. He faced the window and his green eyes glittered in the falling light.

He looked eerily like his mother, and following my earlier conversation with her, I was a little ill at ease. I tried my darnedest to look serene and somewhat aloof.

"Are you feeling well, Julia?" said Gray after he'd arranged his ball cap at the edge of the table. "Something happen today?" He squinted at me.

"No," I forced myself to relax. Lillian had gotten to me but only momentarily. I was going to have a nice dinner with Gray and find out more about the goings on at the farm if I could.

"Sorry. I've just had a lot on my mind," I said.

The waitress came, and we ordered. I had a chicken Cesar salad with fizzy water while Gray had the BBQ beef tips and a Heineken.

Actually, the early dinner was fine with me, as I'd promised Brett I'd join him later in the foaling barn. "What's going on?" I said, fiddling with my napkin.

"Clients early," said Gray, "I want them to look at one of the yearlings we'll be prepping for the sale in July. Then, a few of the weanlings in Barn Two. They want a preview now since they won't get back here until summer. I'm going to sneak them in to see Devil, try to talk them into his syndicate." He smiled. "Then lunch."

It did sound like a busy morning.

"Will you stay?" he said.

The waitress delivered his beer and my water. We both sipped.

I could stay; I'd brought all my research materials, and it was an opportunity to study Brett's cigar box more closely since he refused to let it out of his possession. Plus I wanted to see more of the farm's operation to discern if someone with murderous intent could move about the farm undetected; Gray's foal losses had been going on for months.

"I thought I would, if you don't mind," I said.

Our food was served, and after a few bites, I tried to broach the subject of the foals.

"Has Dr. Bradford . . ."

Gray looked up and grinned. "Tim," he said.

"Tim. Has Tim found out what's killing the foals?"

What the restaurant lacked in décor it made up for in the food; the Cesar salad was very good. I'm especially fond of restaurants that remember a Cesar salad has anchovies.

"No," he said and frowned. "We sent another to the hospital today."

"Has Horace lost a foal?" I asked. Then I regretted it.

Gray scowled at me, and the overly warm atmosphere turned suddenly chilly. "Julia, I've told you Horace has nothing to do with this. It's surely not a premeditated thing. Foals get sick and go down quickly."

He chewed and fumed a little. "It's just part of the business. Sometimes it can't be helped."

I was quiet. Then I said, "What percentage do you think you've lost this year?"

He turned sour. "At this point, maybe fifteen . . . maybe a little less."

"And this is early April. " I left the rest of the foaling season, still ahead of him, unmentioned.

We'd definitely tread into dangerous conversational territory. But, I argued silently, at some point he had to face

103

it—something very wrong was going on right under his nose. If Lillian was correct and he loved his farm and those horses, he'd have to face it sooner or later.

Gray went on. "Julia, you need to understand something. This business . . ." He put his fork down. He was slightly agitated. "There are times when things just go terribly wrong. For no reason."

"I know," I said. There it was again . . . business. So who was right? Was it business or love?

"No, that's just it. You don't know."

We sat eating quietly as the tension built. The television seemed abnormally loud.

Gray wasn't looking at me.

"So explain it then," I said.

"I can't. There isn't an explanation."

The waitress came, and Gray ordered another Heineken. I asked for a coke, my hard-hitting drink.

Gray exhaled. "Look, I'm sorry. It's been a long day, and I'm a little . . . I don't know . . ." He trailed off.

Then he tried again. "Ok. For example. We had a mare a few years ago shipped up to breed from South America. She'd been laid over at a Florida farm in quarantine. She was neglected, and by the time we got her, she was a mess. You could count her ribs. I'm serious. Malnourished. Dehydrated. She was full of ticks and rain rot. She was awful."

He stirred around in his beef tips and took a swig of his beer from the bottle.

"So we had her a while. Turned her out. Fed her. By the summer she'd made her place in the mare's herd. We got her in foal. She was dappled out and gorgeous. So she and another mare are standing under that oak right outside your cottage, you know the one?"

I nodded.

"And a big storm comes up. The tree gets hit by

lightning. The two mares go down, and only one gets up. The South American, she's dead on the ground, and her foal never sees the light of day." He stops eating. "The other one, she's fine. Do you have an explanation for that?"

I didn't.

But I could see how love, in a situation like that, would break your heart.

We finished our dinner quietly with more than a slight tension in the air.

11

Brett was just making his rounds in the foaling barn when I headed over there about ten after nine. Headley, the woman who normally had this 12-hour shift, had gone to Maryland to be with her sister, who'd just had a baby. Having previously worked on this side of the farm, Brett was the logical choice to cover for her. He'd agreed, he said, only when Gavin was able to take over Brett's stallions the following day. Otherwise Brett would be working two days without sleep.

"We got a couple here might go tonight," said Brett when I joined him at the first stall. "This here's a maiden mare, so I got to watch her close. You never know with them."

I looked in and saw a pretty gray mare walking around and around her stall. Her belly was enormous. I looked at the small white card on the stall door, which said that her name was Strafe (Brett said she was by Flying Low), and she had been bred to Parcello, who was also a gray. It was a warm evening, and Strafe was already lathered.

"Yeah, we got a good chance with her," said Brett and moved down the aisle.

Six mares had been moved to this barn since they seemed closest to foaling. Brett said he'd check on Strafe again in a little while, and we adjourned to the air-conditioned lounge, which also served as a dispensary by the looks of the drugs in the cabinet above the coffee pot. There were lots of magazines in the lounge as well as a dartboard, a table, a TV, and a refrigerator stocked with cold water and refrigerated drugs. Brett checked to make sure there were tranquilizers in case Strafe did foal, but, I supposed, was unduly disturbed by the process.

"You can never tell with maiden mares," he said thoughtfully.

I thought the evening was a good opportunity to sound out Brett, especially regarding his nervousness that first day in the stallion barn, which was so unlike the man in front of me who seemed at ease, confident, and knowledgeable about what he was doing; there wasn't a hint of tension in him. I wondered if something had happened to scare him that first day; the answer seemed doubly important since it seemed he associated that fear with the contents of the cigar box.

After Brett finished talking on the two-way to Janine, the other person on foaling duty that night, he fielded my question with some nonchalance, suggesting that his concern had really amounted to not much at all. I didn't press him, and a few minutes later he began talking about it.

"Well, to tell ye the truth," he said, grabbing the iodine from the shelf and placing it next to the cotton, "the night before I did get a little scare."

He turned to look at me, pulling apart the cotton and making neat piles by the iodine. His bony hands worked methodically. "I went to dinner at Jack's Grill in town, and I was driving back in the pickup give me by Mr. Burke."

The farm pick-ups were noticeable because they had the Brookfield name and logo on the side.

Brett was unassuming and respectful; who else but him would call his own cousin "Mr."? I smiled and listened, liking him more and more.

"So I'm coming off the Pike, and behind come this big ole F150, and he's a nudging me along."

"The truck bumped you?" I said.

"Yeah," said Brett turning to grab a cup of coffee. He raised his eyebrows in my direction, but I declined. "Not real bad, just gentle like, just to let me know he was there, I guess."

Still, on a winding road such as the one that runs by the farm . . . that had to be frightening.

Brett looked up at the clock then continued. "But then he tries to pass me, and of course this ain't what you call a big road."

No, the road was not only curving, it was two lanes and without a shoulder to speak of. "Did he run you off the road?"

"Durn near," said Brett. "Sent me into the ditch, nearly."

I asked if Brett felt it had been on purpose, and he said it had certainly been on purpose. "That's the thing," he said, "when he seen me get out of the truck to check on it, he backed up . . . he was coming at me with some speed."

"Brett, did you report this?" I said.

He set his coffee down on the counter and moved to the door. "Best check on Strafe now," he said, heading into the aisle. It had been ten minutes since we'd left her stall.

We walked side by side to the stall. Just before we got there Brett said, "I seen who it was in that 150." He switched on the lights in Strafe's stall and looked in.

"Better call Janine," he said, unhooking his two-way. "She's gonna break her water here pretty soon."

Strafe was sweating profusely and down on her side breathing heavily. In the next second she'd heaved herself up and was once again circling the stall.

She did not look at all comfortable. Two of the mares in the barn stuck their heads out of their stalls and nickered. I thought they sounded encouraging.

"This is Strafe's first time, so she don't really understand what that foal's doing in there."

Pretty soon, Strafe stopped and looked out at us, hung her head, and dropped her front legs on the straw.

"Won't be long now," said Brett. "I just hope Janine gets here or you're gonna have to help me."

Before the festivities began I took one last shot at getting Brett to confide in me.

"Who was in the truck, Brett?"

He looked at me, and fear flitted through his eyes. "I'm just not gonna say right now." He thought it over a few more seconds then added. "If it's all the same to you."

I nodded. Something was scaring him. I wished I knew what it was.

He squirted some hand sanitizer into my palm, rubbed his together, and I did the same. Just then Strafe broke her water and Brett looked out the barn doorway for Janine.

He headed into the stall, pulling gauze to wrap the mare's tail from his pocket. As he moved to Strafe, gathered the hair, and efficiently wrapped it, he said, 'I got to check on the other mares real quick." He smoothed his hand slowly along Strafe's neck comforting her and rose from the straw.

"Keep an eye out, will ye?" he said, and walked off down the aisle.

Well, I said to myself, peering in at Strafe, who was again lying on her side in the straw, at least there's only a few to look in on. I kept my eye fastened on the mare, not

109

knowing what the hell I was supposed to do.

Janine strode in the other doorway and slapped me on the back. "Hey," she said and stepped around me into the stall, bending to kneel before Strafe's birth canal. The mare raised her head and looked back at Janine, then rolled back on the straw.

"Go get Brett, would ye?" said Janine. I guess it was not birth protocol to yell down the row herself; Brett was just a short way off. He was on his cell phone, and as he watched me approach he turned, dropping his head to look at the dirt listening intently; then he headed out of the barn onto the gravel parking pad. I heard him distinctly.

"I know that's what ye said, but I never heard nothing like that from him," said Brett. "No, I'm not saying that." He turned to see me and then said, "I got to go." He hung up.

"Janine wants you," I said, and Brett came back into the barn; that same look of fear briefly rose and disappeared as he glanced my way. I instinctively moved closer to him as we walked the brief distance to Strafe's stall.

"Got to turn the foal," said Janine, kneeling in the straw and peering into the backside of Strafe who seemed quite unconcerned.

"Go on then," said Brett and grabbed a pitchfork. He entered the stall, picked up soiled bedding, and tossed it out next to me. He seemed preoccupied.

Janine, though, had put her hands up the birth canal and was rotating the foal. Soon two wet little hooves stuck out the back-end of Strafe.

"Here she goes," said Janine, and Brett perked up a little. He looked over at me and said, "I helped out over at a foaling barn one time where the owner wanted us to pull that foal outa the mare just as fast as we could." He bent down to peer at the foal's feet and nodded. "Didn't matter

110

about the contractions. Just get that foal outa that mare as fast as ye can, was what he wanted."

Janine had her hands on the foal's forelegs and was waiting for a contraction so she could pull, helping Strafe with the delivery. "Now there's an idea could only be invented by a man," she said.

Brett's big hands pulled the lips back a bit around the foal's legs. I saw a little wet nose lying on the front legs as Janine pulled gently with Strafe's contraction; the mare was breathing a bit and snorting with the push.

"She's doing good for a maiden mare," said Brett in a complimentary way. He bent and very gently stroked Strafe's neck. "You're doing just fine," he murmured to Strafe.

In maybe a half a minute the rest of the foal came sailing out, sopped, glistening, and wetly matted. A little black colt, said Janine. She busied herself with the colt and what surrounded it.

Strafe tried to stand but Brett reached over and very calmly took her head and neck and soothingly laid her back down. "Hey now, girl," he said in low tones, "we'll get your baby up here in a second."

I looked down the aisle and saw three mares leaning out of their stalls nickering their welcome to the new arrival.

Brett smiled. "They can't see this new little guy, but they smell him."

Janine busied herself with the colt, cleared the mucus from his little nose and eyes and let Strafe get a look at him. The mare rolled up enough to get to her foal and began to lick him clean.

Brett grinned up at me. "Best life in the world, ain't it?"

Janine got up and walked out without a word. Brett came next, slid the stall door shut, and said, "We'll get him with the iodine in a little while. For now, we'll let 'em be."

He escorted me out of the barn, and I looked up at him once we were out of earshot of Janine. There weren't many men I'd known who were as gentle as Brett had been with Strafe or as quietly admiring of the miracle of new life. Brett was not an attractive man in the usual sense of the word, but he had a very measured strength about him. And he seemed unaccountably kind.

"Brett," I said, and he looked down at me, "let me know if you want to talk."

He nodded.

"About anything," I said and walked toward the guest cottage beneath a sky filled with stars.

12

The next morning I was up at six-thirty. Celia had acquiesced to Gray's request that I join her as she tended to the brood mares and foals. He was the boss; what else could she do?

I was torn: on the one hand, I had wanted to spend the morning with the Keats correspondence. I'd brought along several books to consult, including volume two of Hyder Rollins's, *The Letters of John Keats: 1814-1821*. This would cover the years in question. The issue was whether or not "Ode on a Grecian Urn" had been composed during a gap in the scholarly record. If it had, then there was a good chance George had the original in his possession.

In my gut, I was sure he had. The facts pointed to it—George was John's copyist and once George emigrated, it was John's habit to send him poems for critique. Why would this ode be the only one John had not bothered to send? It defied logic; all I needed to do was prove it. To myself if to no one else.

On the other hand, I had a persistent feeling about events at Brookfield. Those foal deaths seemed orchestrated, and my mind kept flitting to Horace as the culprit. He had motive, he had opportunity, and by my assessment, he had the temperament. Brett's cigar box was full of tantalizing similarities to the journal, and his fear was real. For a quiet Kentucky horse farm, Brookfield was rife with ominous undercurrents. I needed to see its operations more closely to determine just what those were.

Hyder Rollins would have to wait. This morning I was devoting myself to barns one, two, three, and possibly, four. Vet checks and teasing. That was on Celia's agenda. And mine.

I walked out of the cottage as Celia drove up, my coffee steaming. I glanced to where Brett's house sat, just over the rise; he'd be sleeping by now, having gotten off his shift a half-hour earlier.

It was a beautiful morning, cool though already slightly humid. The mist hung low and blue in the fields; the stallion complex and office below the cottage seemed to drift. Only the black fences were stationary, holding the farm in place. Even the big trees looked ethereal in the blue atmosphere. The world was quiet except for the birds and a lone rooster, somewhere, announcing the dawn.

"Morning," I said, climbing into Celia's truck.

She buzzed off toward Barn One, where Tim's truck was already parked.

Celia got out, and I followed her in. She grabbed her swivel-screened computer from the office in the middle of the barn and met Tim and his assistant at the far end. He had his monitor set up on a rolling table, and Celia set hers on one side of it, punching up a chart. She glanced at the papers secured to the stall. The foals' temperatures were taken each day and recorded there. On a separate wipe-off card was the mare's name, the foaling date, whether it was a colt or filly, and the sire's name. I inhaled the mix of alfalfa, bedding, warm mares, well-soaped leather, and oil as Celia's assistant, Gloria, who was from Brazil and spoke broken English, slid open the first stall door. Wicket had a two-month-old filly at her side. Gloria secured the rope

114

shank across the mare's upper gums and turned her in the stall so her hindquarters faced Tim.

"How long?" said Tim, as he pulled on a plastic sleeve and proceeded to stick his arm into the mare, pulling out fecal material and tossing it into the stall between the mare's legs.

"This is a sixty-day check," said Celia.

Tim pulled and tossed until finally he had a cleared channel. He inserted the ultrasound probe into the mare and with his other hand turned the monitor so he could see it better. The screen looked like black and white static rushing this way and that as Tim sent the probe looking for the fetus. Suddenly there appeared an irregular whitish form.

"See there, Julia," Tim said, pointing to it. "There's the head. The heart."

I saw what looked like the inner workings of a clock there on the screen; a tiny circle filled with rapid, almost mechanical movement, precise and regular. Tim mumbled a string of observations, and I picked up "sound fluid," "good heartbeat," and "filly."

At the last remark everyone laughed.

"Write thees down," said Gloria. "We zee how meny he get right."

Tim withdrew the probe, slid the sleeve off inside out, and moved on to the next mare to be checked. Celia noted Tim's observations on her computer and scribbled something on the stall pad.

I looked out the barn door onto the gravel parking pad. The barn was wide open; anyone could walk in from any direction. I had noticed the same thing the night before at the foaling barn. There was no gate up at the entrance to Brookfield, either. I had heard of a mare stolen from Claiborne, years ago; the thieves had cut and mended the fence so well, no one had noticed. And Claiborne had

115

serious security. Brookfield was a security nightmare.

"Next up is Sojourner," said Celia, and down the barn we went, checking fetuses and looking for heartbeats. When we finished with the seven mares in Barn One, it was 7:25, and we jumped in Celia's truck. Gloria hopped in the truck bed, and off we flew to Barn Two.

I noticed that, except for some of the grooms, almost no one walked from barn to barn. It was also apparent that Brookfield workers all wore the same uniform: blue jeans and a Brookfield-logo polo shirt with ball cap. Though I imagined this was meant as a protective or branding effort, in fact it would be a simple thing to acquire a uniform and gain access to the farm. All anyone needed to do after that was walk the grounds with a sense of purpose. Trucks whizzed by intermittently with hay, equipment, or farm workers in the truck bed; blending in would not take much effort. Like Brett the night before, grooms subbed for each other routinely; no one had mentioned a stallion groom in the foaling barn last night. The farm operated as if it had security blinders on; I'd have to ask Gray about what checks he had in place since, if any were there, I couldn't detect them.

We buzzed past the Stratton Walker where the yearlings would begin exercising, prepping for the July sales a few months off. Celia told me that as spring progressed, they'd be turned out in the evening for the whole night, then brought in from the paddocks, and fed in the morning. After that they'd exercise and be groomed. All the breeding farms worked nearly the same, month to month; it would be a simple thing to merge into the seasonal routine at Brookfield.

The Stratton Walker reminded me of the conversation I'd had with Gray at dinner; I wanted to see the star yearling, the one he was showing to the clients that morning. I made a mental note to get back there by ten.

In Barn Two, Tim joked with Celia and his assistant. It was 7:30 in the morning, and these folks had already been at work for an hour. I didn't feel much like joking; I needed more coffee.

In this barn, Tim stood by an empty stall, and Gloria brought the mares to him. The foals of these mares were old enough to stay by themselves for the few minutes it took Tim to check the moms. Gloria was quick to get the rope onto the mare's gums, Tim was efficient and crisp, and Celia bent over her computer screen, calling out the next mare for Celia to bring and recording Tim's findings on the proper line.

"Ok, this is French Twist. Bred to Mainstay," said Celia. "Might be a good one." Tim had his hand up within inches of a possible high earner.

He tapped his monitor. "Strong heartbeat. Good fluid." Tim called out the measurement for the fetus, took a picture, and slid out his arm.

"Who brought the donuts?" he asked, as Gloria led in River City, and he slid on another sleeve and went up her hind end. Pretty soon the ultrasound probe inside the mare slid around looking for the fetus. Seconds passed. I glanced at the monitor but saw only static. Tim adjusted the screen to a more upright position. Everyone got quiet.

"How far is she? Tim said.

Celia checked the computer. "40 days."

I saw a small white blob come into slight focus. Tim stopped swiveling the probe and stared at it. It seemed inert.

"Dead."

You could feel the emotions drop. It got even quieter.

"No heartbeat," said Tim briskly. "Is she on Regu-Mate?"

Celia checked. "Yes."

It was so quiet all of a sudden.

"Undersized."

"OK," said Celia.

"Check her again in four days."

Tim packed up. No one said anything, and we moved on to Barn Three.

I thought about the dead fetus. Gray had said there were ways to kill a horse that evaded detection; I wondered if the same was true of a fetus.

The mares in Barn Three were all doing well; Tim and the crew completed their tasks in short order. He packed up and headed out to his truck and I decided to ask about the foal—and now fetus—deaths.

"Tim," I called, walking out of the barn as he latched his truck. "Can I talk to you a minute?"

He squinted at his watch. "Naw, sorry. Don't have the time right now. What's up?"

I wasn't quite sure how to broach the subject. Like Brett, I just had a feeling about events at Brookfield. I needed to see if any of my suspicions were at all well-founded.

"I wanted to ask you about the foals . . . the ones that died."

His smile faded. He looked at the ground. "Yeah."

The concern he showed made me think that perhaps I wasn't as out of line as I'd thought. "Is there anytime later maybe we could talk?" I said. "Just for a few minutes?"

He pulled at his cap. "What would you like to know?"

I thought for a moment about how to approach the subject with Tim; I didn't have a right to intrude into his business.

Finally I said, "I'd like to learn how the farm works, and I know Gray said you were looking into the losses. I

118

thought talking to you would help me understand the situation." That seemed an innocuous enough answer.

Tim hesitated, studying me. "How about five o'clock?" he said, looking at me steadily. "I have to be back to check on a foal later. I could stop by, after, at the cottage."

We agreed that five would be fine. Tim jumped in his truck, his assistant got in the passenger side, and they sped off.

Celia and I drove to the stallion barn to pick up the teaser, Shagan, who stood placidly in his stall. He was an ugly, short, thick-necked, big-headed, coarse-looking stallion, and his job was to determine whether or not a broodmare was ready to breed. However, said Celia, there was a catch: though he approached broodmares as ready to breed as any other stallion, he was never allowed to finish the job.

"I know he's ugly as sin, but really he's worth his weight," she said, explaining that in the old days "teasing" a mare was essential; nowadays veterinary medicine took over that task. "But I'll tell you the truth," said Celia, pulling gently on Shagan's forelock, "nobody's gotten rid of the old ways. I don't know a breeding farm in Kentucky doesn't use a teaser." She reached to the side of Shagan's stall and grabbed the halter. Then she smiled. "Be careful what you do in this life or you might come back one of them," she quipped.

She put the halter on Shagan and I asked about her daily routine. Yes, she said, it was regularized; horses fared better if you did the same thing, in the same way, at the same time, every day. They were creatures of habit in the extreme.

"Of course, something always comes up—lacerated fetlock, some fool yearling runs into a fence, foal goes down, colic—the usual stuff, so you can't always keep to your schedule."

She clipped a stallion lead on Shagan and walked him out to the truck. I followed and climbed in the passenger side as Celia got in behind the wheel, feeding Shagan's lead through the window. Unmindful, he stuck his big head in the truck's bed snuffling for grain.

"So anyone could figure out where you were going to be at any given time?" I asked.

She yanked Shagan's head out of the back. "Oh, sure. We all know where everyone is pretty much all day." She patted her two-way. "We can always get ahold of whoever we need to." She folded Shagan's lead up until he was a few feet off her window. "It's pretty much the same on all the farms around here. People tend to do things the way it's always been done."

We took off, and Shagan trotted contentedly beside the truck—plop, plop, plop—and forty-five seconds later we arrived at the barn.

Again it struck me that anyone could be in and out of these barns in a matter of minutes. Brookfield, like all breeding farms, was organized to maintain a predictable routine. Every day and every season, employees did the same thing the same way with as little variation as possible. If you'd worked around stud farms in Bluegrass Country, Brookfield's routine wouldn't be hard to figure out. If you knew how to kill a foal, you could gain access to the barns easily. If you knew where the syringes were kept, getting the ugly job done would take no time at all. Gray's lack of suspicion about his losses seemed odd given it seemed the appropriate and obvious response to me.

We led Shagan into the barn, and beside stall one I noticed that from the underside, he might have been mistaken for Devil the day before. He was as masculine as they come, at least from that angle. He stuck his ugly head in toward the first mare, who promptly pinned back her

120

ears, barred her teeth, and ran straight for him.

"Pregnant," said Celia succinctly.

Shagan dutifully plodded to the next stall. This mare looked blandly at him as if he wasn't there.

"Not hot," commented Celia. She wasn't making any notes, so I guessed she was able to keep all this information in her head.

We went on down the aisle; some mares kicked the stall doors. Thwack. Some turned their backs, some tried to bite him, and a few spread their legs, urinated, and "winked" their vulvas.

To those last Celia said, "Hot."

Other than the mares in the stalls, there didn't seem to be anything standing in the way of an intruder and the young foals.

After Shagan's duties, he trotted back to the stallion barn at the side of the truck.

Gray was just coming out of the breeding shed with Brett as Celia and I were exiting. It was eleven o'clock, it was unseasonably hot, and it was time for lunch.

"Did your clients see the yearling?" I said to Gray as we met.

"They loved him. Knew the mare."

He said they'd look in again on him when they came for the sale in July. I'd missed watching the yearlings, having been preoccupied with the big-headed teaser's workload.

"Did you hear anything about the foal?" I said to Gray as we met.

He looked confused. "What foal?"

"The one who went to the hospital."

"Oh," said Gray. "He died."

I was beginning to understand Gray's comment at dinner. Sometimes things didn't make sense.

Like the events which would unfold later that night.

13

I spent the afternoon at the guest cottage with books and papers spread across the mahogany dining table. Laptop to the right, window blind pulled up to catch the view, yellow notepad before me, pen in hand; I was ready to tackle Hyder Rollins' collection of the John Keats correspondence. Gray's clients had decided to return after lunch, and later in the afternoon a man from a nearby breeding farm was to visit Devil; Gray hoped he'd send some mares Devil's way next season. That evening Gray had a meeting.

I was on my own for the foreseeable future.

First, I set out my list of dates for George to my left. Next to this were the 1819 dates of composition for John Keats' odes: "Psyche," April; "Nightingale," May; "Urn," middle of May; "Melancholy," middle of May; "Indolence" is listed as "spring," 1819; "Autumn," likely prior to the end of September. General scholarly agreement exists that all the odes were written between January and September of 1819. What I was looking for, then, was confirmation that sometime following the last of April a letter was received by George from John that did not include "Urn," followed by the same sort of letter that included "Melancholy." This would indicate that John either did not send George an original of "Urn," or that the letter, which presumably included the poem, had been lost. Of course it might also be true that John had not followed his usual procedure of sending his brother poems or that George came into possession of the original in some way other than by letter (such as in his 1820 trip to England).

I worked on, searching through the published letters looking for clues about the ode and George's finances. I found nothing about his fortune but a lot about how he'd absconded with money from John, which their sister and others complained about. There was also information about the poems.

Since the odes were composed in 1819, generally from January to September, I focused first on these dates. I knew from general scholarly material that "Ode on a Grecian Urn" didn't appear in any of the letters—but I could've cared less about that. I was looking for large breaks in correspondence during this period, which could mean that there was poor-quality letter delivery or that John Jeffery's handling of the letters had resulted in the original ode's absence in scholarly collections. And that's exactly what I found.

The famous letter from John to George of February to May, 1819 contains "Ode to Psyche," among other poems. The next two letters to the George Keats' are dated September and November of this year, thereafter there is a letter to Georgiana Keats dated in January of 1820 during George's visit to England.

Since John always sent George his newly finished poems, he would have sent his brother "Ode on a Grecian Urn" between May and September. Such a letter, however, is missing from the scholarly record. Either it was not written, I concluded, or it was lost or suppressed by Georgiana's second husband, John Jeffery.

There was also the possibility that George, during his 1820 trip to England, received this ode from John and copied it since the earliest record we have of the ode is George's 1820 version.

Though there wasn't any definitive proof that George had acquired John's original, kept, and preserved it, my instincts made me absolutely positive this is exactly what had happened.

Looking out the window, I noticed low clouds gathering and rolling toward the farm. It looked as if a storm were brewing out there. I went out to the porch and was met with a cool breeze. The air smelled like rain, and the paddocks and pastures gleamed green. To my right, up on the rise, a herd of mares and foals grazed without concern—a slowly undulating bay mass. Ahead of me was the tall, spreading oak under which the ill-fated South American mare had perished.

I glanced at the herd with a bit of concern.

The scene was calming. I was used to the city—to squealing car tires, sirens at all hours of the night, to drunks at 2 a.m.—so the quiet on the farm was unsettling. There were scores of horses around me; how could it be so quiet? Other than the stallions' response to mares in heat, the atmosphere was usually filled with a serene, slow, quiet calmness.

Thunder struck, a portent of things to come. The herd to my right, startled, galloped across the grassy paddock as one. At the far end they slowed and bent once again to graze.

I went inside, and the storm passed over.

But another one hovered just over the horizon waiting for dark.

14

At five, Tim knocked softly on the cottage door, and I joined him on the porch.

"Shoulda gotten that rain," he said, looking at the sky to the south. "Need it already."

We sat comfortably, me in the rocker and Tim on the chair to my right. He had soft brown eyes, and for a man who reportedly worked ten to twelve hours a day he was surprisingly upbeat.

"So what can I tell you?" he said. The smile faded quickly as I mentioned the foals.

"I know you've been trying to figure out what killed those foals. I wondered if you'd found anything."

Tim looked skeptically at me, not sure whether to talk to me about farm business or not.

I went on. "Gray says the deaths are just a normal part of the foaling season. I don't know anything about your business, so I wondered if you felt the same way."

He relaxed. "Well, he's right. You never have a perfect foaling season; you'll always lose some."

"But you are trying to find out what caused their deaths?"

"Yeah. The foals we lost weren't insured so they

don't need a necropsy report—it's just me at this point."

I must have looked confused, because Tim continued.

"Insurance companies don't like to pay off without a report from Rood and Riddle's diagnostic lab. In fact they require it." He went on. "Given the financial situation Gray's in, since these foals weren't insured, there was no need for the extra expense." He paused. "So we decided to look into it ourselves."

I was uncomfortable with the next question.

"OK, but let's just say . . . hypothetically," I began. Tim looked at me, alert and serious.

"What if somebody was actually doing this to the foals or that fetus today, the one you found was dead. I guess what I'm asking is could somebody be killing them and it not be detectable?"

"Did Gray say that's what he thought was going on?" said Tim, now clearly concerned. "Because he hasn't said anything to me."

"No, he hasn't suggested it."

I didn't know what else to say. My uneasiness was either founded or not. I just hoped Tim would feel comfortable enough to be straight with me.

He took his time answering. "Ok. Here's the thing. There are several ways to kill a horse that, if you were any place else but here, *would* be undetectable. Like, for instance, say you were in New York, where I used to work, you could get away with it. There's just not the world-class facilities there to catch things you'd see real clear here in Kentucky." He stopped. "What I'm trying to say is it would be fool stupid to try something like that here because we have the best pathology lab, literally, in the world."

He looked me in the eye. "You just couldn't get away with it."

"But you aren't sending these foals to the necropsy

center."

Tim nodded. "No."

"So," I said, pressing the issue, "if someone was foolish enough to try it, is there a way to kill a foal or a fetus, or even a stallion and not have it be easily detectable?"

"Yeah, there is." He sat back in his chair and looked out over the paddock, talking but not looking at me. "Actually there are several ways."

I was quiet.

He spoke softly. "For example, there are two types of penicillin—potassium penicillin and sodium penicillin." He turned in his seat and looked at me as he spoke, his eyes darkening. "If I have a foal needs penicillin, I always send home sodium with the owner because you won't overdose a foal on that." He seemed to be justifying himself, and his face had turned very serious. "But if you don't give the potassium type by I.V. very, very slowly, it's real easy to overdose a foal and kill it quick as hell."

He sat back. "Thing is, you'd see that come up in the tissue, then you'd look to see why that foal was on penicillin—was there an infection, was there some reason to give it . . . ."

"And you haven't found that?"

"Naw," he said, sounding somewhat perplexed. "Nothing like that. No trace of it."

"And then there's Chlorhexidine," he said. He had begun to speak with slight agitation as if these possibilities were things he'd been turning over in his mind for some time. "That stuff is sold to farms by the gallon. We use it for everything, it's an antibacterial agent. You can scrub up wounds with it, sterilize stalls . . . hell, I use it on mares before I check them."

A tractor rumbled by, and the overall-clad driver waved. The mares took flight again in the paddock to our

127

right.

"So what's wrong with it?" I said.

Tim cracked his knuckles. "Thing is, let's say you're out in a field somewhere, and you need to put down a horse, and you don't have anything with you to do it." He looked at me somewhat bleakly. "You can always use Chlorhexidine. It works pretty well."

We sat quietly, though we both felt the weight of an unspoken concern. Celia drove by in her green truck. Tim looked at his watch.

"So do you think somebody could be doing this?" I said, putting the question to him directly.

Tim chose not to answer. "There's also insulin. That stuff, if you overdosed a horse, would look just like a heart attack, just like the potassium . . . or you could use prostaglandin on a mare. "

It seemed the possibilities were mounting.

"You mean a pregnant mare?" I said, meaning like the one with the dead fetus earlier in the day.

Tim shifted in the chair and again looked at his watch, clearly becoming uncomfortable with the conversation. "Yeah, I'm always concerned about leaving that stuff around. A disgruntled employee, anyone really, could get out in a field at night with the mares and just get rid of all the best mares' foals pretty quick."

I asked what prostaglandin was supposed to be used for.

"You short-cycle a mare with it," explained Tim, reducing the normal 21-day cycle by about five days so they could be bred sooner. "You give it to a mare you want in heat."

"But if a mare's already pregnant," he said, "up to 45 days, one shot will kill the fetus."

The mare earlier in the day had been pregnant only forty days.

I asked one more time. "Do you think someone is killing these foals?"

Tim shook his head. "Naw, I don't think so, Julia. There's no reason."

Maybe he was right, I thought. Or maybe there was a reason, and he had his arm in it up to the elbow.

15

A little while after Tim left, there was a soft knock at the door. I opened it and squinted out onto the back of Lillian's head. She turned quickly at the sound of the door.

"Just wanted to see how you were doing," she said, holding out a bunch of her prized tulips and irises.

I opened and stepped back, and she glided in.

It was much darker in the guesthouse than outdoors, so I busied myself at the window, screwing open the rest of the blinds, then crossed to the table and tried to make some order. I was still a little embarrassed after our previous conversation. I had to admit she'd hit a nerve. Besides, I had too much on my mind at the moment to examine feelings she'd alluded to about Gray—I hadn't missed her point.

She seated herself at the table as I worked, smoothing her cotton skirt and just being patient with me.

"I came to apologize, Julia," she said.

"No need," I retorted quickly, still not meeting her eyes. "Not a problem."

She reached out and put her hand over mine, and I went still.

"It's all right, Julia," she said quietly. "I'm not one

to share secrets."

She smiled.

What secret could she be referring to? I wondered.

"I have enough of my own," she said and patted my hand.

It was difficult not to like this woman.

Finally, I sat down across from her. "I sent off the form you signed," I said by way of clearing the business end of things and reestablishing some sense of equilibrium between us. Maybe even friendship. "But you're already certain about the painting, aren't you?"

"Yes, of course. I'm quite sure it's authentic," she said, and her tone meant there was no further need for pretense between us. "And in our present situation whatever money it might bring, even if it's not much, would be helpful."

I hadn't thought of that, but she was right of course. I didn't know how much a real Audubon "sketch" would be worth but certainly something substantial. I guess "not much" is a relative term. We'd find out soon enough.

"What are you doing with all these books," she asked then, looking around at my notes and open books and my laptop. "If you don't mind me asking."

I wasn't sure what to say. That I was nosing around in her family's history? That I was wondering if her distant relative had defrauded the family? That I was trying to prove otherwise? Given Lillian's reluctance to talk about her father, I felt she'd be much less welcoming of my inquiries into his antics and those of her more distant relatives, so I decided to . . . prevaricate. Again. The Burke's did not bring out the best in me, it seemed, mother or son.

She had her eye on printouts of George's journal entries. "Those look interesting," she commented, noting, I supposed, the dates.

"Yeah," I said, straightening them. "Just some

research I brought down with me from the university. Can't seem to stop working." I finished and patted them into neat 8 X 11 inch stacks.

"You know, Lillian, I do have a couple of questions," I said rather earnestly, hoping to deflect her attention from the stacks and books, some of which had the name "Keats" prominently displayed on their academic spines. I shoved them aside, turning the pages toward us and the spines and tops away.

"About Gray and what things were like around here when he was younger?" I wondered what my fishing expedition might land.

She caught my eye, and I saw she knew I was trying to change the subject. Gracious as she was, she complied without comment.

We spent the next hour talking about Brookfield as it was in Gray's youth. It sounded like an idyllic youth to have had: 4-H club, riding bareback at full speed over hills and valleys, colorful stable silks, camp-fires . . . A wholesome, honest way of life. Lillian mentioned days filled with breeding, foaling, weaning, sales, and races. All, she said, directed by Gray's father, a man at the top of his game who'd earned respect throughout Bluegrass Country. And by the time of his death, she added, in England and Europe as well.

"Yes, it was a really glorious and rather glamorous life we led back then," said Lillian. "Not bereft of heartbreak, certainly, but glorious all the same." She lifted her eyes to the hills outside the window. "The sport of kings, it's called." She looked back at me. "And some days, it was just that."

My visit to the Seelbach's Rathskellar came back to me, though, and I wondered about the darker side Gray had mentioned, and especially about Shorty, the man Gray had said trained all the runners for Brookfield.

"That does sound wonderful," I said slowly, "but what about the other side of it, the terrible stuff you read about. Jockeys having to throw up all the time, and the terrible things they did—and still do—to the horses. Was that ever a part of Brookfield?"

The light in Lillian's eyes seemed to dim at my question. "Oh, yes," she murmured. "For a short time. We didn't put up with it, of course, once we found out."

She seemed to think a moment. "You did meet Horace and Miriam, correct?" She asked it as a preamble, it seemed to me. I nodded.

"I've known Miriam since she was a little girl. Oh, you have never seen a child more beautiful than she was— that coal black hair and that fair skin—she nearly glowed. A lively little sprite and the apple of her father's eye. He was our trainer—Shorty was what everyone called him—and he was the very best in the business. He was a tiny man, wiry, but smart and fast, and with an eye that saw everything. Nothing got past that man when it came to a horse. He had a gift." She sighed. "Shorty . . . I have not thought about him in years."

I waited a little for the memories to settle. "Do you know what happened to him?" I asked.

"Oh." said Lillian, as if she'd just recalled he'd gone. "That's right. No. I do recall that Miriam was a little girl still, and when Shorty disappeared, which was quite a surprise to all of us, her family from Ireland was here visiting, and they took her back with them. We didn't see her for a number of years. And then . . . ." Lillian seemed to be trying to see into the past. "And then as I recall, Horace," and here she looked up at me and tilted her head thoughtfully, "back then was really a very different man than he is now."

I wondered, did she mean he wasn't a complete ass back then? But I held my tongue.

"Back then he was much more self-assured." She grinned at me. "And of course much slimmer."

Personally, I couldn't picture it.

"Yes, he was not so . . . oh, what's the word?"

I had a word.

"Pompous, I suppose you'd say," she finished finally. "Not quite so pompous." She thought a moment. "I think being made to feel small makes one try to look so much bigger than one really is."

Well, I thought, that may be true. But as for me, Horace was an ass and he would always be an ass, big or small. It didn't much matter to me.

16

About nine o'clock I heard the sirens.

Lillian had gone home some time before, and I'd settled back with a book feeling grateful she'd come. I read and mused about the Keats mystery. Once again, I missed having Albert at my feet, as is our habit.

At the sound of the sirens, though, I put down my book and quickly went to the window. An ambulance raced up the driveway and veered to the right, heading over to the stallion complex.

Lights were on outside one of the barns shining on the gravel, spotlighting the ambulance as it pulled to a stop, and two white-clad men hopped quickly out, heading inside.

For one second I thought about calling Lillian, but instead I grabbed my jacket and went to the door. By the time I'd gotten through the cemetery and was on the gravel, myself, the attendants were wheeling a figure strapped to a gurney quickly to the back of the vehicle. Even with the covering, there was a lot of blood.

I began to run, and as I did Gray came out of the barn and trotted to the ambulance just as the doors closed and the siren took up its alarming wail.

One part of me felt relief, and one part was scared to death.

Other grooms came out, and I heard the stallions as I drew closer, stomping and sounding their uneasy response to the unease in the air. Devil then appeared, led by a grim-faced Richard who quickly deposited him in a stall on the other side of the barn.

"What happened?" I said as I approached Gray, who stood with his hands on his hips staring after the ambulance, which had already been gone some minutes. He looked lost.

"The police are on their way," he said. Then I saw his eyes. Confusion. Fear. Disbelief. He was stunned.

"The police? Why?"

Still Gray hadn't moved. He seemed unable to move.

Behind him Richard and Juan began closing the barn doors. A few other grooms switched on more lights. This was odd.

Where was Brett?

"Oh my God," I said. I looked after the ambulance, then back at Gray.

Why had Devil been moved out of his stall?

"Gray?" I said quietly.

He finally jerked, as if coming awake, then walked over to the fountain and sat down heavily in the soft light of the spots shining up through the water.

"Gray, please tell me what happened."

In the distance I could hear another siren.

Gray didn't seem able to speak. I looked around. Richard was still attending to the barn, but I didn't want to leave Gray sitting there by himself, so I turned back and just waited.

The siren was drawing nearer.

"Was it Brett?" I said, finally.

Gray hung his head. "You would have thought Medes." He looked up at me bleakly. "That would have made some sense, at least."

Again I asked. "Gray, where is Brett?"

He was silent.

"Devil got him. In the stall." He couldn't say more.

"Will he be ok?" I said. I wanted assurance I knew he couldn't give. There had been a lot of blood.

Gray's face didn't betray him, but his lip trembled. He took a deep breath.

"I wish I hadn't seen him," was all he said.

The police arrived. Two of them. They got out of the car slowly and walked toward us, talking to each other. They had notebooks and flashlights, phones at their hips. They asked to speak to Gray alone, and he got up and walked toward the barn with them, leaving me sitting on the fountain bench. One of the men continued to talk with Gray while the other wandered off to speak with one after another of the grooms. The officer then came over to me and asked if I'd seen anything, if I'd been out of the cottage during the evening, and then turned toward his partner who was still with Gray. He excused himself and joined them.

Next Richard slid open the barn door for them, and I watched all three head into its interior; then one of the men went into the stall with measuring tape and a camera. He came out shortly, got halfway into the car, and with one leg stretched to the gravel, I overheard him call for the forensic team.

Did that mean Brett had died?

Eventually Gray recovered enough to come over to the fountain. I stood, and he put his arm around me. We stood there, just outside the circle of barn light, watching silently as the policemen roped off a perimeter around the barn, checked the floor inside the barn, checked the

137

walkway around the barn, and then went to talk to the other men and women who showed up shortly in a van. They spread out and took pictures and notes and talked to the grooms again. Finally one motioned for Gray, and he reluctantly left.

Richard walked over, rolling the t-shirt sleeves up over his biceps.

"Do you know where they took Brett?" I said.

"Memorial."

"Can I go?" I wondered.

"Ride with me if you like." Richard was usually low-key and pleasant.

Not tonight.

Memorial was a hospital like most others. Out front was a curved lit entranceway and short, concrete walk up to the double-wide electric doors. Inside it was bright and antiseptic but not too crowded. Ten-thirty: too early for Friday night disasters.

The floors down the hallway were so clean and shiny they seemed to swim before my eyes, or perhaps, I thought, I was just feeling disoriented. Richard and I sat in the emergency room on a nondescript blue-patterned couch, waiting. I asked the receptionist a few times if we could talk to the doctor. She asked me if I was related to Brett, and I lied and said he didn't have any living relatives. This being Kentucky, her graciousness was in keeping with traditions there; she didn't ask about insurance. Perhaps Gray had mentioned something to the ambulance attendants. She didn't let me talk to the doctor. He was attending to the patient.

An hour or more passed. Neither Richard nor I felt like talking. Richard left and returned with a bottle of water. I tried not to feel anything.

Finally I called Lillian; she'd already spoken with Gray. I told her I'd keep her informed about Brett; I'd call

138

as soon as I heard anything. She wanted to come to the hospital, but I didn't know how long it would be, so I told her to sit tight.

Another forty-five minutes passed, and I got up again to ask a passing nurse about Brett. She didn't know anything.

I waited until midnight, thinking surely by then someone could tell us something. I approached the receptionist, again. She was polite and said the doctor would come out when he could. She seemed used to this. I was not.

Finally I tried talking to Richard.

"Do you know what happened?"

Richard shrugged and slumped next to me, very unlike him. "Gray found him."

Really, I thought. That was odd. Gray had clients and then a meeting in the evening.

"He got me on the two-way. He'd gotten Devil out of there. I took the stallion." Richard sipped the water. "Made the mistake of looking in the stall."

My stomach turned.

Richard sat up. "The whole thing doesn't make sense," he said.

"Why?"

"There was no reason for Brett to be even near Devil's stall. Gavin took his stallions because Brett had the foaling last night. He had the rest of the day off."

Richard turned to me. "And there was no blood on Devil's hooves."

I felt a chill. "Did you tell the police?"

"I did."

A few minutes later the doctor came out, buttoning up his doctor's coat. He checked with the receptionist, then motioned Richard and I over to a couch in the corner. The one out of earshot of the others in the waiting room.

He sat facing us, his hand resting on the top of the couch. He had on polished Cordovan slip-ons and, now, a clean doctor's jacket.

"I'm Doctor Conrad," he said. After a brief few seconds he continued, "Your friend has been through a lot."

Richard and I stared at him, not saying anything.

"We operated. I apologize for not being out here sooner, but I didn't want to tell you something until he was out of the OR."

Dr. Conrad swiveled and crossed his legs. He looked concerned. "I am not optimistic. He has sustained massive injuries. His head trauma alone is quite serious, and he is dealing with other difficulties—breathing, the injuries to his back and kidneys, so . . ."

"When will you know?" I said.

"I can't say," said Dr. Conrad. He was frank and looked directly at me as he spoke. "He's in our ICU, and if he makes it through the night, I anticipate he will be there for some time."

Dr. Conrad stood. "You can call if you like. Of course, we don't allow visitors in the ICU. He has no family, did you say?"

"Well," I equivocated. The doctor looked surprised. "He does, but they are, uh, otherwise engaged." I stood, too.

"Well," said Dr. Conrad, "I'd be happy to speak with them."

I got his message.

"We'll do our very best. I'm sorry I don't have better news." Dr. Conrad concluded the interview.

Richard and I sat for a few moments, not knowing exactly what else to do. Finally, Richard decided we'd better leave; he had to be up working at 6:30, and there wasn't anything I could do sitting there in the waiting room. We left, feeling empty and frightened.

On the drive back, Gray called Richard on his cell

phone, and Richard told him what Dr. Conrad had said. I talked to Gray for a moment; he was still with the police but felt they were winding up, and he'd wait for me at the guest cottage. He'd let his mother know the news.

As on the drive out, Richard was silent on the drive back to the farm. It gave me time to think. Time I didn't really want because I wasn't happy about the thoughts that came.

Someone had tried to kill Brett, that was very clear. They'd tossed him in Devil's stall hoping to finish the job and have it appear Devil's work. That had backfired, leaving the obvious—someone, probably someone on the farm, had tried to murder Brett.

It appeared, also, that Gray had possibly lied about his agenda for the evening.

I shook my head. This was ridiculous; I was really getting melodramatic. There was an explanation for Gray's change in plans, or else the meeting had adjourned early. What was wrong with me?

We arrived at the farm and turned up the drive.

I put aside these thoughts. I was simply upset and worried about Brett, which accounted for my undo suspicions.

I was also afraid.

When I entered the guest cottage, Gray was at the dining table amid my books, notes, and the laptop I'd left on when I'd grabbed my jacket and run out the door hours and hours ago. He looked tired, as I'm sure I did. He got up, put his hands in his pockets, took them out, and gave me a hug, which I sorely needed. We went to the couch and sat heavily.

I told Gray a little more about the doctor's comments, and he nodded. Neither of us wanted to speculate about what the morning might bring. I looked at Gray and was a muddle of feelings, not all of them linked to

Brett. My heart went out to Gray. He looked miserable and still in a state of shock. But I was also confused and needed time to sort through the events of the night. Who, exactly, had tried to kill Brett, and why? In the end, desire to comfort overcame my confusion. I squeezed Gray's hand gently and he relaxed.

Sitting there watching his grim look and the pale cast to his complexion, I reminded myself that of all things helpful to Gray and Brett, a muddled, uneasy mind was the least of them. Gray's hand had regained some warmth. "Did the police find anything?"

Gray said they'd just nosed around and asked a lot of questions. He had accompanied them as they searched the barn area, then roped it off, and went through Brett's little house, which apparently had already been searched by someone. If the police found anything, they'd kept it to themselves.

"They are considering this attempted murder."

I guessed Richard's comments about Devil had been born out by what the police found. At least the stallion would be ok. I just hoped the "attempted" part would remain the charge.

"Who do you think could have done this?" I said.

Gray's head was down; he stared at my hand covering his but said nothing.

"Why would anyone do such a thing?" he asked.

I felt sure I knew the answer to that. "For the money."

Gray rubbed his right eye. He seemed beyond weariness. "You really think there's something to this thing about my grandfather?"

"Actually it's your great-great grandfather, and yes, I do think there's something to it." That's all I felt comfortable saying. After a few more minutes, Gray said he'd better get some sleep since the farm work would start

142

up at dawn, no matter what had happened tonight. He stood to go. I was surprised that I didn't want that to happen. I dreaded being alone just then.

"I'll certainly understand if you want to get back home," he said and turned to the door. Then he turned back. "But I'd really appreciate it if you could stay." He sighed. "I really would. I can get somebody to come stay with you if you'd like."

Dread and confusion aside, I had no intention of leaving. I had a good three more days here, and I wasn't going to leave until I knew that Brett was all right. There was a bit of not wanting to leave Gray mixed in there, too, if I'm being honest. I also had in mind getting a peek into Brett's house.

I wondered if his box was still there.

I escorted Gray to the door, and he pivoted to me, looping an arm around my shoulder. I said I'd be there in the morning, and he seemed relieved. "Good," he said. "That helps." Then he turned the knob and was gone.

The next morning a stallion shank was found wedged under the stone fence at the far end of one of the yearling paddocks. One of the workers, retrieving a colt early that morning, had noticed it and picked it up on his way back to the barn. If there were prints, it's possible he obliterated them. The three feet of heavy metal links plus most of the twelve-foot leather strap had been gathered up and secured in red Vetrap. A length of leather was left unwrapped. I was told there was a lot of blood and flesh on the gauze, spatters on the exposed leather shank, and that the bits of hair stuck to the weapon were straw-yellow.

I thought it strange the weapon had been left in so obvious a place.

It was apparent that the weapon Brett had been beaten with came from the stallion barn; I'd seen the same sort of lead rope being used on Devil. Unlike other leads, the stallions' had that longish section of heavy metal links, which gave the groom both control and options; I'd seen a groom control the fractious Medes by letting him mouth his shank. That the weapon came from the stallion barn reinforced my feeling that whoever had attacked Brett was certainly associated with the farm and quite likely was familiar with the stallion complex.

Horace again leapt to mind.

He had an interest in a number of the stallions, had been associated with the farm for years, knew all the employees, and had easy access to any portion of the farm.

Plus he was nearly out of money.

Horace or possibly someone else I hadn't been alert enough to think of. What I didn't know was how many people might have overheard Brett talking about his blackened cigar box. Who might have befriended him, sympathized with his confusion over its contents, and when Brett proved unwilling to turn it over, attempted to take it from him?

It could be almost anyone.

It could even be Gray.

17

I hadn't wanted to consider that. Gray wasn't supposed to be anywhere near the barn if what he'd told me at dinner was true. He'd had clients, and showings, and meetings, and was supposed to be busy the whole day. I also wondered what he had being doing sitting at the desk when I came back to the cottage. How long had he been there, or what's more, *why* had he been there? To see me or to nose around in my research?

But Gray was the victim, I reminded myself, not the villain. He had no reason to kill his own horses. Or Brett. What purpose could that possibly serve?

I knew if I was going to get to the bottom of this, I had to look at all the facts dispassionately. With at least a semblance of objectivity.

So yes, I had to consider the possibility that Gray could have orchestrated all the havoc wreaked on both the horses and on Brett—but to what end? How would that help his financial situation? The most obvious way was by money gained from insurance, but Tim had said the foals weren't insured. I mentally crossed that one off my list. Perhaps he was trying to lure Horace into making an offer. I didn't know the history between them—perhaps Horace had been reluctant and Gray was attempting to make Brookfield appear a steal. Of course Gray might be desperate enough to want Brett's box to puzzle out the mystery himself. It all might boil down to money. Gray certainly did need money.

The darker reason, I realized, might not be financial at all. Perhaps Gray actually resented being burdened with the responsibility for Brookfield. Maybe this was all his attempt to get back at his father—guilt, hatred, and anger are a great recipe for bad acts. Lillian had said Gray's father had been fierce. Stern enough to push his son over the edge? It had happened before.

Whoever had attacked Brett, it was personal. And the attack was driven by rage. Brett's face had been rendered a pulpy mess, or so Richard had said. Was Gray angry that Brett wouldn't share clues to the Keats' lost fortune? Had Gray finally lost control when Brett refused him one last time? Though Gray had scoffed at Brett's ideas about the box, he also said he wouldn't show it to anyone. Was that why Gray had befriended me, because he knew I'd studied Keats? It wouldn't have taken but a minute to call up my bio online at the university; my entire academic history is there for anyone to see.

Was this all a set-up?

I fervently hoped these thoughts were on the wrong side of the argument. I felt they were, but I had to consider any one of them might be the truth.

It couldn't be Gray, I insisted one last time. It just couldn't be him. But, of course, it could. It could be almost anyone.

18

Notwithstanding the night's events, early April was still the busy season for Brookfield. The day's schedule was filled with breedings at nine and two, vet checks and teasings, turn-out and feedings, and of course foalings coming at all hours the night, plus the odd problems that no one predicts.

I had a lot of time to wander around by myself. The first thing I'd done was call the hospital. Brett's condition had worsened during the night. He was listed as "grave." I didn't like the inference. I asked if I should come to the hospital but was told Lillian was there and they would inform the family if his condition changed. I left all the phone numbers I could with them, just in case they relented, made sure my cell was fully charged, and headed out.

I wanted to get a look at Brett's house.

Of course the police had taped it. It was part of the crime scene. Though I felt slightly apprehensive about crawling in the back window, I did it anyhow.

The air was close inside, and the bedroom seemed, at first, dark due to the bright day I'd just left. When my eyes became accustomed to the dimness, I stepped over the pile of clothes and around the mattress that had been hauled onto the floor, heading into the living room-kitchen area, where Brett and I had met so recently.

It had been searched, as Gray had mentioned the night before. The contents of the cupboards were all over the counters and tiled kitchen floor, the couch was overturned, and the cushions slashed. Even the saltshaker had been emptied onto the kitchen table. The place was a mess, further proof that someone had been after the contents of Brett's box; he had nothing else of value to steal.

I stepped into the living room and, trying not to disturb anything, peered around the horse magazines strewn on the thin carpet. I picked through the horse and racing photographs that had once hung on the walls. Fingerprint powder graced some of the debris but for the most part the living room was a jumble of hurriedly tossed belongings. There appeared to be no cigar box in the mess.

There was something I recognized, though, pinned just under the overturned couch arm. It looked like a photograph of a bird. I eased it out and flipped it over. Yes. It was Brett's grandfather's Florida postcard to his friend Jacoby "over to the Seelbach," as Brett had described. A wave of sadness came over me as I remembered Brett's attempt at humor. I looked around me. Brett was a good sort, an honest person who didn't deserve this.

I tucked the postcard in my jacket and kept looking for the box. But I didn't find it.

When I'd accepted Gray's offer to stay at the cottage, he'd invited me to accompany him to Keeneland Race Course on Saturday to watch two Brookfield juveniles begin their two-year-old campaigns. I was to meet him at eleven since post time was 1:15. In view of last night, I seriously hoped he would not be going. I met him at the office hoping he was going to cancel, but he had no
148

intention of missing the "babies" races.

"Please don't feel you have to come," he said, packing up the folders on his desk and flipping off the TV monitor on which he'd been watching race film. "I completely understand if you want to skip it, but I have to go. I have part interest in them, they were bred here, and these babies are the future of our stallions." He stood and slotted the folders in a black spiral on his desk. "You know what that means to the farm," he continued. "If they run well, they might end up like Lock 'N Load, Aury's three-year-old who's due to run in the Wood Memorial pretty shortly. If he does well there, he might actually get in the Derby."

I didn't feel at all like going to a race.

"He won't *win* the Derby," said Gray, now talking to himself. "But I'd sure like to see him run in it."

I thought it over. What would I do around the farm? I'd gotten what the intruder had missed at Brett's, and I wasn't sharing that information with anyone. Sitting around the hospital wouldn't do anyone any good. I didn't feel like following Celia around all day, or Richard. My research had been completed yesterday; I wanted to wait until Brett was better to share my findings with him. And I'd like nothing better than to ferret out the truth about Gray's involvement in all this, so the logical option was to go. We headed out to the Navigator. I felt nothing but grim determination.

On the way over, we both tried our best to talk of anything but the events of last night. I received a Kentucky Bluegrass lecture from Gray. Keeneland Race Course, he told me, is a horseman's horse park; even the term "course" recalled America's racing antecedents at the old English tracks. Keeneland's rich history and its setting—in the middle of Kentucky Bluegrass Country (the richest thoroughbred breeding area in the world, I was reminded)

149

and its proximity to one of the premier breeding farms in Kentucky history (the old Calumet Farm is right next door, I was told)—made Keeneland home to some of the most knowledgeable horse people on the globe. I had read that Keeneland sales are regularly attended by Saudi Arabian sheiks, Irish horseracing giants, and multi-millionaires from around the world.

Gray added that he'd been at the sale when a single yearling sold for over ten million dollars. This, he said, is not a surprise to breeders who willingly pay $500,000 to breed one mare to a stallion like Storm Cat. Well, he corrected himself, they had when times were good. Horse racing, like everything else, was subject to economic ups and downs.

As I was learning close up and personally.

Gray's comments helped me understand why had such hopes for Aury and Schism. The stud fees and yearling sales figures he recounted were sorely needed to support the farm.

He wanted to show me the track itself before we took a look at his horses. We could have gone to the clubhouse, but he wanted to sit out where he could see his "babies," so that's what he showed me. The grandstand faces west, not east as in most other tracks, but its racing schedule—in early April and October—makes the warm sun welcome. When we emerged into the stands, the track and infield spread open before us with its hedge carved in letters spelling out "Keeneland" in well-kept trim. The black and white furlong poles and unassuming rooflines seemed to fall away as calmness spread over me. Looking out over the track, I understood why Gray had mentioned Jack Keene in admiring tones, noting his dream to create a place where his beloved Kentucky horses could run. That's what they are born to do, Keene and countless others who joined and followed him felt. It's what they devote their lives to, quite literally, from dawn to well beyond dusk, as I was learning.

I had recently become painfully aware of the darker side of racing, and I checked my cell phone in response to these thoughts. The drugs, the cruelty, the harsh decisions, the losses of life were all part of the "game," as some called it. Here, looking out on the serene simplicity of Keeneland, I felt something else—the purity, the joy of grace and strength in athletic expression was also part of racing, and Keeneland seemed an expression of that tradition. I recalled watching the chestnut and bay mares graze in the paddock and understood a little of why people devote themselves to these horses. Now, standing next to Gray, I felt part of a nearly palpable heritage devoted not to money, not even to competition or winning, but to beauty of form and to spirit. That's what hovered over the simple dirt oval. That's what I saw in Gray. That recognition. The love of that tradition and the love of these horses he wished to preserve and continue.

"Do you want to go round back to see the babies?" he said, breaking my reverie. He stood and stretched.

Gray pointed out the winner's circle we passed, commenting that it had been constructed for Queen Elizabeth when she'd come to the inauguration of a race for fillies named after her. It was a half-oval with a low iron and simple fieldstone fence. For larger races, he told me, awards were presented in the infield so everyone can see the horse, the jockey, the trainer, and owners. Things now were much different than in the old days when the winner's circles were chalked in the dirt for every race. He said if Antienne's filly came in first, he'd haul me over there, too.

I said I'd be happy to go.

"The babies" were saddled and walking as we approached the paddock and to my eyes seemed big as the Derby horses. It was early in the two-year-old campaign, and the fillies were probably ahead of the colts, so Gray was here to watch a filly by Antienne hopefully break her maiden.

"If she wins today it might be a while before her next race," Gray said. Enough of these babies have to win to make a field for "winners of less than two races," the next one she'd be eligible for. *If* she won, Gray reminded me. The other horse he'd come to see was out of Ataway Raj, and he said he'd take a win from either one. Depending on how they ran he wanted them in a graded stakes race next.

If one of them won, he reminded me again.

The first filly, Waltz With Me, was light of bone and elegant. She had a finely shaped head, long thin legs, and was tapered and tucked up, with a high tail set. She was a deep chestnut and, I thought, quite beautiful. Gray's eye was keen, and he thought she moved well, had a calm but alert, intelligent eye, and he hoped for very good things from her.

"She's like an Ethiopian runner," he said, "tall and very athletic, and I think she'll be a good route horse. She's no Ruffian," he said. "I just hope she's fast." He turned and looked down on me. "There's nothing like speed."

There were a lot of other people in the back, some taking notes, some just quietly looking over the field.

"If she does well I'd like to see her at Saratoga in August." He put his arm around my shoulders. "Hell, she might go to the Breeders Cup." He was leaning forward now, pressing toward the grandstand.

"If she wins," he qualified. "If she wins going away."

He was trying to be realistic.

We went to our seats for the start of the race. There were eight fillies moving toward the gate at the chute set up on the far side of the track to our left. Gray thought if she did well in the 4.5 furlong race over the Headley Course, he'd suggest the GII Darley Alcibiades Stakes. Here at

Keeneland, he explained, but nearly twice the distance.

"Well, we'll see if she can run first." He was trying, in the vernacular, to rein himself in.

The fillies began loading into the starting gate.

The crowd was composed of mostly trainers, owners, and folks there to check out next year's Triple Crown hopefuls. There was not the tension I thought would be in the air, just an expectant, observant excitement. These were Kentucky folks, well-used to the ups and downs of the game; everyone recalled the stallion raced one too many times, due to retire to stud in a forty million dollar syndication, who'd snapped his leg a furlong after the wire. As Gray had said, sometimes things just didn't make sense. Still, hope is an odd beast, and the truth was, everyone was hoping to see and hopefully buy into the beginnings of a great career; I could see it in the faces all around me. Though they knew how unlikely it was to find a superhorse among the fillies, in the back of everyone's mind was the fact of Ruffian, Go For Wand, Zenyatta, so everyone was willing to keep an open mind. It could happen. You just never know.

The field was loaded at the chute just off the main track; they settled in the gate for a moment and then they were off. They broke well, and Waltz With Me stayed in the middle of the pack, running easily with the others. This was a half-mile race so it would be over quickly. Soon the field began to stretch out, the frontrunner pulling off a bit, with two others tucked in behind her. Waltz With Me was now well off the rail on the outside in fourth place.

Gray looked pleased.

At the turn for home the front-runner started to lag, and the two tucked in behind moved up to overtake her, running neck and neck. From the back of the pack a dark bay filly began to weave through, settling in just behind Waltz With Me, who was still holding her position off the rail. She was now in third place as the former leader faded further back. The dark bay went wide and pulled up beside Waltz With Me. Just then Gray jumped a little, bumping into me and letting his binoculars flop on his chest.

"Did you see that?" he said. "She got a look at that bay. Did you see her?"

Next thing I knew Waltz With Me was charging forward, moving between the two front-runners though there didn't seem to be much of a hole there.

"Wow!" said Gray, now visibly excited.

They were into the stretch, still running three wide. Waltz With Me, again, surged forward and as the wire loomed ahead, kept extending her lead, adding more and more daylight between herself and the rest of the field as the wire neared.

"She's rolling," said Gray, and the people around us began to cheer as they saw Waltz With Me pull farther and farther ahead. She ended up winning by a length and a half, and Gray was beaming.

The fellow next to me was on his feet pointing with his program. "That's an athlete you got yourself out there."

Gray replied happily, "Yeah, she's got a little Donnaguska in her."

For a moment we'd both forgotten the troubles we'd left behind at the farm.

"My phone will be ringing off the hook when we get back," he said. "I bet I get calls for $150,000 on her."

"Would you sell her?" I asked.

He didn't think about it a moment. "Maybe."

We were about to head over to the winner's circle when my phone rang.

It was the Lillian. Brett had died at 1:16 p.m., about the time Waltz With Me had crossed the finish line.

19

Lillian reported that he'd never regained consciousness. Gray sank down in the grandstands seat when I told him, deflated and horrified, as people around us hurried from the stands to see Waltz With Me head to the winner's circle.

I felt angry. It hadn't occurred to me that Brett would die. I'd considered it, of course, but not with any real seriousness. Now the reality settled in as, around me, people chatted, wrote down numbers, made studied observations to their neighbors about the prospects of various mounts; it was all suddenly surreal and offensive.

Gray was likewise stunned; he stared out onto the dirt track unblinking and then, without emotion, said we'd best get back as quickly as we could.

I don't remember the drive. Marcy was pale and quiet as we entered the office. The hospital had called there looking for Gray so she knew about Brett. They had wanted to know about funeral arrangements.

He didn't have anyone else, so I asked Gray if he could be buried on the farm. He'd already thought of that. There was a place up over the hill, a nice grove of crab apple trees that bloomed every spring; Brett had liked it there.

Marcy called the hospital, and I went into Gray's office, closed the door, and sat down.

I noticed a dark-framed box over his desk. I hadn't noticed it before. Gray came in and saw me staring at it. There was a picture of a man and a woman and in the middle of them, a horse. In the bottom of the box were three dried roses.

"That's the memorial service for Seattle Slew," he said. "I was there. I picked up those roses; they were all over the place." He sat down in the dark leather chair in front of his desk, making a tent with his fingers. "It was a twilight service." He paused a moment, looking at the box on the wall. "I was sitting there and happened to look up. You know how mourning doves usually roost at night?"

He looked at me but seemed deep in recollection, so I just nodded.

"When I looked up, the stars were just coming out, and there was a little sliver of moon, and all of a sudden about thirty doves rose up out of the trees, all at once, and just flew off into the night."

"Gray," I said, "I'm going to find out who did this."

"They just flew off into the night," he said still looking at the horse, remembering.

Marcy knocked tentatively at the door then peeked in.

"Sorry," she said. She looked frightened. "The police are here, and they have a search warrant."

I got up.

"And they asked if you were here, Mr. Burke."

Gray strode out the door and immediately entered into quiet conversation with one of the policeman.

I neared the waiting room myself and heard the policeman reading Gray his rights. He was being placed under arrest.

156

He turned to Marcy and asked that she call both his lawyer and John to make sure things were covered on the farm; then he turned to me. "Call my mother, would you? I'm not sure what's going on," he said, and they led him to the patrol car.

Gray walked through the door between the two policemen; it occurred to me bleakly that he actually might be found guilty. I'd gone over the evidence myself, and I could understand—if you didn't know Gray, if you hadn't seen him at Keeneland—that it might look bad. He'd lied about his whereabouts to me, he needed money, he stood to inherit if Brett's little box provided clues to the fortune he'd thought it might. There was a mounting circumstantial case that Gray was guilty.

But spending the day with him, seeing his genuine love for the horses and the life he felt responsible to preserve, my instincts convinced me of his innocence. And since he was innocent, someone else, someone I felt was very close by, was guilty.

Back in the cottage I thought through who it might be. People do strange things when pushed to their limits, I knew, things even they don't think themselves capable of. Horace needed money. He had opportunity. The stallion barn, in fact the entire farm, was as familiar to him as his own home; he knew the nuances of schedule as well as the horses' quirks and peccadilloes.

I brooded, wanting to prove what at present appeared only possibly true.

I sifted through the photocopies of George Keats' journal, hoping to find solace or answers among his entries. Struck once more by the man's industriousness year after year in the face of the odds against him, I hoped the integrity and perseverance George had shown was reflected in how Gray was meeting the vagaries of his own difficult situation, over a century later.

One that was becoming more difficult moment by moment.

I called Gwyneth. Suddenly it seemed vital to learn more about Horace and his financial problems. Gwyneth didn't answer her phone; it went straight to voicemail. I left a message for her to call, and mentioned it was urgent.

I walked to the stallion complex, looking for Richard; perhaps he knew something about Gray's arrest. The stallion manager wasn't in the breeding shed so I walked over to the first barn, noticing Chaney in a beat-up green truck on the gravel, a load of bagged grain in the bed. I unlatched the barn door and heard the gravel crunch and felt something touch my back. I turned around. Chaney had let down the truck's rear gate, backed up, and now hard metal pressed against my chest. The fact that he was purposefully trying to hurt me took seconds for me to realize. Just before he could, I dropped and rolled under the gate. I caught Chaney's face in the rearview mirror; he was laughing.

Richard came out just then and I straightened and brushed myself off. He shook his head and shrugged, realizing what Chaney had done but said nothing. He nodded at me and returned to the barn. Who knows what Chaney might have done had Richard not ventured out just then?

Though I was tempted to give in to my anger at Chaney's actions, Richard's response made me feel it was just Chaney being his usual, harassing self. No harm, no foul, was the way his stunts were viewed at Brookfield.

I caught up with Richard as he closed the stall door and headed on to the next to muck it out.

"You heard about Brett?" I said.

He had. "Service will be tomorrow, I guess." Richard looked up. "Monday would be difficult." His South African accent was slight, but he did clip the last word more than usual.

The barn was cool; someone had forgotten to turn off the overhead fans. Still, my neck was damp beneath my hair.

I asked Richard if he'd heard that Gray had been arrested.

"I figured it. Because of what Chaney said." Richard had a wide-tongued pitchfork; he entered Aury's stall and tossed bedding aside in the center revealing a large, wet circle. He deftly scooped up the damp bedding there and tossed it in the small trailer I was standing beside.

"Could you brush that bedding back in?"

I picked up a broom from the trailer's back end and swept up around the entrance to the stall.

"What did Chaney say?" I said.

"Said he saw Gray and Brett arguing around 6:45 when he came down to turn out the stallions."

I thought Gavin had taken that over for Brett. "Arguing about what?"

Richard set the pitchfork down outside the stall, slid it shut, and latched it.

"Don't know." He said he didn't hear that. Just heard them yelling at each other.

That didn't sound like Gray. Or Brett, for that matter. I followed Richard to the next stall, which usually housed Medes and which Richard slid open and walked into. The stallions were out in their separate, two-acre paddocks.

"Do you think Chaney is lying?" I said.

His head down, Richard kept talking. "It's not my place to say. I've seen some strange things. Stallion took the nose off a guy once, a guy who'd been around horses all his life. Unlikely things occur. Never seen this, though."

Richard's response to the situation seemed to be to keep working.

I could relate to that; it was my own way of coping.

Which is why I was frustrated. There wasn't a thing I could prove, at the moment. It appeared to the police that Gray was guilty of, or at least potentially involved in, a series of abhorrent crimes, but at the moment, I couldn't prove his innocence. Horace, on the other hand, who I felt could be guilty of the same crimes, remained enigmatic. I knew that George Keats had possessed an original copy of his brother's most famous ode, but I couldn't prove it, and I couldn't find it. I knew that George had secreted away enough money to support his large family, but I couldn't prove that, either. I knew Brett and Gray's grandfather had probably been living on that money, but I had no way to prove it or find the money. Most frustrating of all, there was a killer somewhere very close, and I had no idea how to discover who it was.

I paced outside the stall as inside, Richard just kept working. Patience, as Gwyneth has often pointed out, is not one of my virtues.

The next day the farm staff met in the crabapple orchard at eleven o'clock to bury Brett. That hour was chosen because the farm operated on a schedule where, barring an unexpected calamity, everyone was given lunch between eleven and noon. John, the farm manager, had asked a local minister to preside over the burial and so it was done, simply and efficiently, with Lillian in attendance but without Gray since he was still in custody. He would have to pay his respects in private, if and when he was released.

To his credit, Brett, though unschooled and unsophisticated, was well-liked among the employees, and nearly all showed up to bid him farewell. They stood around in Brookfield shirts, jeans, and ball caps. No two-ways went off, and in general the service was subdued and dignified. After it, everyone left but me.

160

Gwyneth had yet to return my call. I put in another and got her on the second ring. I explained the events (she was dutifully consoling) and asked for help. She said she'd call me with information if she had anything to report but couldn't get to it until later that night due to her own work load. She'd put a copy of her findings behind Rachel, the terra cotta cherub in my office, in case I returned home before she contacted me. I thanked her, asked her to give Albert a hug, and sat on the grass beneath the crab apple next to the fresh grave.

There was not yet a gravestone since the burial had been so quickly arranged. Just a simple piece of fence board and the churned, mounded ground showed where he lay. I planned what flowers I'd plant. I didn't make any promises or cry.

But I would find the person who had killed him, and if it were possible, I'd also complete the task he'd set himself, to—as he understood it—clear his family name.

The next morning while I was in the shower, Gwyneth called leaving a cryptic message on my cell phone. Her findings were as follows: Horace had no prior arrests, no civil cases pending or in the past having to do with gambling or any other financial debts; he was known to frequently place bets but apparently had never welched on one. He'd been active for many years in breeding at Brookfield and at other farms both here and abroad, and had been married to Miriam for more than two decades with no legal separations or court interventions of any sort on record. He was, for all intents and purposes, squeaky clean.

Gwyneth was thorough, so this information was quite depressing. But "squeaky clean" only meant publicly, so I'd look into where Horace was the night of Brett's attack.

First, though, I'd try to clear Gray's name by

speaking to the person I'd been avoiding, the person who'd implicated Gray directly.

Chaney was the last person I had interest in approaching, yet he might hold the key to either clearing or further condemning Gray; alternatively, he might shed some light on Horace's whereabouts the night Brett was attacked. I didn't think him of sufficient ambition to have committed the crimes himself, but he certainly was capable of foul play and very well might be involved or at least know more than he had told the police.

Not knowing whether Chaney was working or not, I ventured down to the stallion barn just after lunch and found Richard in the barn housing Medes, Aury, and Devil. He said Chaney had been pressed into service on a daily basis since Brett's death; they hadn't found a replacement yet. He'd be in Barn Two, which housed Antienne and Circuit Breaker—the barn where I'd first encountered Chaney. That seemed a long time ago now.

He was forking rye bedding into the stall as I approached and ignored me.

I stood in the aisle, quietly waiting for him to acknowledge my presence, which after some minutes he still had not done.

"I'd like to ask you a few questions," I said. Even though he'd tried to hurt me, or, who knows, perhaps even cut me in half with the truck's tailgate, I was not leaving without the information I needed. It was not in my nature to let go of a problem once I'd dug in to solve it.

"So?" he said, and kept to his task, not looking in my direction.

"I understand you told the police you heard Brett and Gray arguing the night Brett was attacked."

Chaney didn't respond.

"I'd like to know a bit more about that," I said.

"What for?"

I picked up a broom thinking to help him brush back the bedding as I had assisted Richard. He turned and sneered. I put the broom back.

"I'm just trying to understand what happened that night," I said, attempting to keep my tone neutral.

The barn was warming; Chaney flicked the overhead fan and resumed shifting the bedding around in the stall. He straightened, turned, and stared at me. His blue eyes were cold.

"Joined the police force, have ye?"

An appeal of my friendship for Brett would not elicit information from this man. Nor would an appeal of friendship for Gray. I opted for appealing to Chaney's mercenary spirit, as it seemed the only sort he might actually possess.

"You know if Gray goes on trial for this, your job would be in jeopardy. The farm might not sustain his absence and the blow to its reputation." I let that hang in the air. "You might well lose your job."

Chaney leaned on his pitchfork. He seemed to consider what I'd said.

"Lose my job, huh?" he said sarcastically, then chuckled unpleasantly. "Do you know how meny years I been workin' around horses?"

By the look of him—hard, slim, wiry, and in his late fifties—it could well be over forty years.

"Ye think I'm here outa sum sort of desperation, is that it?" He cocked his head at me, with no little menace.

"No," I said, "of course not. I only meant that finding out who killed Brett would go a long way to putting this farm back on its feet."

"Ye think I care a lick about that?" Chaney laughed. "I could walk off this farm right now, an' get on nearly enyplace I'd like, afore lunch."

I had insulted and angered him, which did not bode

well for extracting information.

"Ye think these God-damned Mexicans have everthin' locked up real tight, dontcha? Got all the God-damned jobs, and the rest of us are jus' scraping along, glad as hell for enything enybody gonna give us?"

He took a step toward me, and I became well aware that we were alone in the barn.

"No," I said, as emphatically as I could. "I'm not concerned about your petty fight with the Mexicans." I'd had enough of his intimidation. "Or anyone else, for that matter. I couldn't give a good God-damn if you worked here or went someplace else."

He looked startled for a minute then smiled.

"All I want to know is what you saw and heard the night Brett was beaten."

He stared, and I stared right back.

"Ye think your gonna get your boyfriend off, is that it?" He snorted. "Yur a regular investigative reporter," he said, chuckling. "I seen you around here, pokin' your nose in, talkin' up Brett all nice, being squired around by the boss." He shook his head. "Yur a piece a work."

"What happened that night?" I said flatly.

He walked past me, brushing my shoulder so I lost my balance. He hopped in the golf cart pulling the rye bedding, drove up the aisle to the next stall, hopped out, slid open Antienne's stall, went in and began mucking it out. I followed on foot.

"I'm not leaving until you tell me what you saw that night," I said, standing in front of the stall as he tossed soiled bedding towards me.

He stopped. "All right, I'll tell ye."

He stood in the middle of the stall; behind him in the corner were dark shadows. This stall was exactly like the one in which Brett had been placed. I put down a slight shiver as Chaney began speaking.

164

"I'd come over to check on Medes, on account a his feet. I had turnout, en Richard said I needed to check on Medes, so I stopped by over there, jus' before. Gray an ole Brett were goin' at it pretty good. Yellin', cussin'—never heard ole Brett so upset." He smiled as if the remembrance pleased him.

"What were they arguing about?"

"Dunno," said Chaney. "I jus' heard Brett accusin' the boss-man of wantin' ta steal that crap-filled cigar box of his. He jus' kept shoutin' about it."

"Then you do know what they argued about."

Chaney smiled at me. "Well, I guess I do, now that ye mention it."

"So what did Gray say?"

"He denied it."

"What did he say, exactly?"

Chaney pulled on his chin, as if in deep thought, but he was simply ridiculing me.

"Let me recollect here a minute," said Chaney. He stood in the stall for quite some time as if in thought.

I did not say one word.

Finally, "He said he did not know where that ole boy got his information from, but he was only tryin' ta help."

"What information?" I said. It sounded as if Brett had heard something about Gray's intentions prior to their meeting.

"Dunno." Chaney resumed mucking. "I jus' told ye everythin' I know."

I wanted to press him but Chaney had gone back to his work, refusing to look at me. After a bit, I realized he'd effectively erased me from his universe.

I thanked him stiffly and walked down the aisle toward the barn door.

"Hey, girly" he called after me, "hows about a little

165

truck ride after I git off?" I heard him chuckle.

I continued out the door, my back ramrod straight.

Two o'clock found me sitting in a slatted rocker outside the cottage soaking in the afternoon, which had turned a bit cool after the unseasonable warmth the day before. I'd been thinking over my conversation with Chaney and Gwyneth's scant findings, feeling no closer to clarity than I had the day before. I wondered about the phone call Brett had received that night in the foaling barn: I tried my best to recall his exact words. He'd commented about what the person on the other end had said, but insisted that he had not heard the same information from "him." I wondered who the "him" might be—Gray? Horace? I mentally added Chaney to the list. The night Brett was attacked Chaney said Gray referred to "information" Brett had gotten wrong; perhaps the two conversations were connected.

But how?

I was also aware that time was running out; my classes resumed in two days and I'd have to either ask Gwyneth to cover for me, or head back to Cincinnati shortly. I decided to decide that issue later.

I was again feeling overwhelmed. I'd collected quite a lot of information regarding George Keats, Brookfield Stud, and Brett's murder, but I felt no closer to understanding any of it. It had been my intention to collect my Keats notes, review them, and take another look at the words on the Florida postcard, but I couldn't seem to get myself out of the rocker and off the porch.

So it was that I was stretched out there when Gray drove up a bit after two-fifteen, my legs sticking out and dug in at the heels, rocking only slightly every once in a while. There was a bottle of lukewarm water on the whitewashed batten boards next to me. Gray got out of the

166

Navigator slowly, not having even stopped below the cottage to check in at his office; he didn't say anything but just sat down on the wicker chair to my right and sighed.

We talked about small things: Brett's funeral service, about who had been there, what the minister had said, and when the grave marker might arrive—some weeks, said Gray, since he'd ordered a nice one.

"Why did they release you?" I asked, wondering how that had been accomplished. Had he been cleared?

Instead of responding, he said, "How would you like to come over to my house?"

Gray didn't spend a lot of time there; his duties on the farm took up most of his days and evenings over three-quarters of the year. I was interested in seeing it, especially now, since there might be information there that would shed light on events in his past.

"I'll make you dinner," he said and smiled. He rose and put his hand out to help me up.

I felt torn; on the one hand, I would be relieved to get away from the farm for a little while, and I did want to unearth whatever I could about Gray's family. I looked at him and felt familiarly conflicted. Part of me wanted to be with him, but another part was reluctant. Though I was convinced of his innocence, I wasn't a fool. Plenty of very bad people seem the nicest guy on the block to their neighbors. Accompanying him would isolate me from help should I need it. And, in the event my instincts were correct and Gray was just as he appeared—one of the good guys— removing myself from the farm meant I couldn't observe the employees or farm activities. If I hoped to find Brett's murderer, I needed to be on hand not off eating dinner at Gray's house.

In the end, I agreed. I decided to ask Gwyneth to take my classes; if I ended up not needing the time, I could easily let Gwyneth know. When I called her, I'd also make

167

sure to let her know my whereabouts for the evening. I asked for a few minutes to change clothes, wash my face, and unbeknownst to Gray, give Gwyneth a heads up. Gray waited in the Navigator.

On the way to his house, I asked about his arrest.

"How did you get the police to release you?"

The late afternoon was a pretty one, and the drive, with the early April trees budding out, was lovely. The rolling hills, the greening fields, the grazing horses . . . Bluegrass Country had a very strong appeal to me.

"There wasn't enough evidence to charge me," said Gray. He added wryly, "They mentioned I shouldn't plan any trips in the near future."

I noticed Gray had not answered my question directly.

"But they asked you what happened, right?" I wondered what had passed between Gray and the police.

"What did you tell them?"

"I just told them the truth, " Gray said. He was a man of few words when he wanted to be.

Undeterred, I pressed on.

"Which is?"

Gray glanced over at me assessing whether I was inquiring or interrogating him.

He turned back to the road. "I'd run into Brett earlier in the day, when I had the clients looking over Devil. Brett seemed anxious, and I asked him what was going on."

I nodded because Brett had also seemed anxious to me.

"So he said he just had an uneasy feeling that he was being watched and sometimes followed. He also claimed he'd heard something about me, which he wouldn't elaborate on. He just seemed scared."

"Right," I said, remembering his story about being run off the road and his cryptic phone conversation the

168

night at the foaling barn.

"You noticed it, too?"

I said I had.

"I couldn't talk to him then, I had these clients. I thought he'd be turning out the stallions so I said I'd meet back up with him then. Which I did."

Gray turned off the two-lane blacktop into a smaller gravel lane, and then a few hundred yards up he turned left again up a drive lined by trees.

"It's just up ahead," he said.

Brett must have thought it important to talk to Gray, I concluded; he hadn't needed to be at the barn at seven. "So what did Brett say when you met up later? Richard said there was an argument."

Gray raised his eyebrows slightly. I guessed it was still a marvel to him how fast news traveled on the farm.

"He was worried about that cigar box of his. I told him to give it to me, and I'd put it in the safe in the office."

"And Brett wouldn't do it."

Gray nodded and pulled up to a semi-circle in front of what looked like a nondescript concrete building.

"Well," he said, putting the SUV in park, "he didn't want to let go of the box. Which I thought was ridiculous. If he was frightened and felt he was being followed because of it, why not put it in a safe place?"

Yes, that made perfect sense. I'd been through a similar conversation with Brett myself. He probably would have felt more uncomfortable without the box in his possession.

"So we did argue a little, I guess."

"Did he ever tell you what he'd heard about you?"

"Naw, couldn't get him to talk about it. Just that cigar box."

I was pleased Gray's explanation was so clearly plausible; perhaps, I thought, simply telling the truth to the

169

police had effected his release.

I just hoped it was enough to secure it.

"And I did not prevail. Brett refused to let go of that box," said Gray.

He leaned forward and put his left forearm on the wheel and his right hand around my shoulder, pulling me to him. I closed my eyes and felt his left hand gently on my cheek as he kissed me.

"I've been wanting to do that for quite a while now," he said, pulling back after.

I felt very comfortable, too comfortable. I needed to sort out the dark events whirling around us both before I could even begin to make sense of anything happening between us.

And I still wanted to hear the end of Gray's explanation.

I smiled to acknowledge the kiss.

"How did it happen that you were the one to find him?" I said. I ran my fingers lightly over the top of his wrist and let it settle on his forearm; there seemed to be two conversations going on at once.

Gray matched my smile. I have to say, though, his had a slightly sarcastic cast to it as if he knew my mind was on the murder, and I was just trying to be polite.

"I was exasperated. I told Brett to think about it, that I had some work in the office, and that I'd catch up with him in an hour or so. I wanted him to think things through."

He opened the door, but paused before getting out. "Of course when I went back to meet him, he was already . . . ." He left the last to my imagination.

20

Gray's house was actually made of smooth, gray concrete, which was not at all what I had expected. It was at the same time contemporary yet, weirdly, a seamless part of the landscape. He'd had an architect influenced by Ando design it, he said, though the interior was completely Gray's own vision. After entering, we walked a narrow hallway that very quickly opened to the right into a long, rectangular room with a wall of windows overlooking a flagstone patio set with a fountain. The room was lined with books and horse photographs, as well as a comfortable-looking leather couch, chairs, and a low, narrow table. In one corner was a computer and wooden file cabinets below a large desk; the room functioned as Gray's study and in-home office.

To the left was a door to the kitchen and then a glass block wall-opening to the kitchen for pass-throughs to the rectangular study/office area to our right. Off that room, farther to the right, was the master bedroom suite. We walked straight ahead and then down two steps into the great room with its two-story open living area, walkway across the top to the guest rooms on the second story, circular upward stair to the left, river-rock fireplace with a huge portrait of his father, mother, sister and, I supposed,

Beau Lyons, or some other famous horse, over it. The furniture was mostly primitives with Oriental rugs scattered on the planked wood floor, and behind us was a state-of-the-art kitchen with an eating and serving bar at the top of the steps. There were two seating areas: one right in front of the fireplace and one slightly to my right that looked out over the patio. The walls to our right and left were filled with windows, and there were vertical windows to the sides of the fireplace. There was a lower level as well but I thought we could save that until later.

I just wanted to flop down on the leather couch in front of me and take in the beautiful green light, the low bubbling fountain and planted urns on the patio. I was also thinking of how I might gain access to the computer. I wanted to search the Brookfield website and see what I could find out about Horace's fat fingers in Gray's financial problems. I figured there would be less online protection here than at the farm itself.

I looked at Gray and smiled. He wouldn't like my plan. Not one bit.

He smiled back and asked if I'd like a glass of wine.

Dinner was delicious, in part because it was completely prepared and served by Gray. I find a man who can cook and enjoys it a rare pleasure since those virtues, like patience, are not in my repertoire.

We began with field greens and feta, dried cranberries, and a few toasted pine nuts dressed with balsamic vinegar and a good olive oil. Next came grilled Coho salmon, asparagus wrapped in bacon, and tiny boiled new potatoes complete with the center peeled stripe. It was simple, lovely to look at, and, as I said, delicious. Especially given the addition of a big chardonnay as an accompaniment.

We watched the light change from the late afternoon spring green to a dusky blue tinged with peach at twilight. The interior lights came on automatically; Gray dimmed them and lit candles on the coffee table where we'd shared our dinner.

"I do have one of those thin, dense chocolate cakes, if you like, for dessert," he said, leaning back on the couch with his glass of chardonnay.

Please, I thought. The man bakes.

"Mail order," he said. "But from New York."

I passed. We sat in silence, an oddly comfortable one, given the circumstances. I looked at the family photos arranged on the gate-leg table set against the near wall and wondered about Gray's sister, featured in several of the shots. She resembled her mother, and, as with many of the pictures, was often posed on or around a horse.

"What's your sister doing there," I asked, pointing to a framed photo in which she appeared to be falling off a smallish brown horse, her head along its belly, her arm nearly touching the ground.

Gray rose, retrieved the picture, and pointed to a red and white cloth on the ground just next to her outstretched hand. "She was always doing stuff like this. She was a great rider, here see—she's picking up that kerchief." He smiled. "We raced around the farm like that all the time."

The sun had fully set, and it had cooled down quite a bit. Gray held the picture with both hands in silence. "Now, I hardly get on a horse," he said and put the picture back in its place.

He headed to the fireplace, and I noticed the chill in the air; early April evenings can be downright cold in Bluegrass Country.

"Would you like to see some other photos of my family?" he asked, crumpling paper and stacking wood for a fire.

"I'd be happy to," I said. Maybe I'd learn something

that might conclusively clear Gray.

He piled albums on the coffee table and turned up the lighting. We started with pictures from childhood and moved forward. His mother and father looked strong, healthy, and outdoorsy. As might be expected, in most pictures there were horses. His mother had big white teeth and a pageboy; she looked vastly different than at present with her gentile, upswept do and finely sculpted features. His father was big-boned with thick brown hair like Gray's. His sister grew up before my eyes, and I felt a lingering desire to know her in person as Gray flipped through her childhood and young adulthood.

"This one has pictures of the wedding. I guess you don't need to look at those," he said, setting aside the album.

"No, I'd like to," I said, taking it from him. I flipped it open to the portrait of Gray's sister and her husband on their wedding day. They were dressed formally and looked straight into the camera, happy, as they should have been on that day.

"They look so happy here," I stated the obvious.

"Yes, we were all happy back then," said Gray. His mood had darkened.

"Have you visited them in Italy?"

He looked out at the patio, dark but for the lighted spots on the fountain and urns.

"I joined them just after they'd moved there five years ago." He looked back at the picture. "I'd just gotten there in this photo." He pointed to one with the three of them standing before a smallish Cessna. "I only had a little time. " He looked at me. "Breeding season," he said and smiled lopsidedly. "So I got over there for a week, and that was pushing it."

I sat quietly. Sometimes people talk if you just allow them to.

Gray sat back against the cushions. "We went to the Uffizi, we ate, we bought vinegars and some wine." He trailed off. "We were on the beach most of the time, though. It was beautiful." He laughed a little. "I wanted to see where Tesio lived and bred his wonderful horses. I badgered them mercilessly." He stopped for a moment. "Lake Maggiore, in Northern Italy. I just wanted to stand on the same soil he had." Gray looked at me, I think to see if I understood this at all. "You know what he said? Tesio? *A horse perseveres with its heart and wins with its character*. That's a quote."

It seemed to me that could be true of most of us.

"Anyway, they told me to go on ahead, and they would fly to Rome. They accused me of not being able to get off the farm no matter how far away I got from it." Gray smiled, and I took it that his sister and brother-in-law had been joking with him.

"What are their names?" I said.

"Amelia and Josh." He looked at me thoughtfully. "Maybe you'll meet them sometime."

I'm sure I didn't blush, but something I did made Gray look away.

"Yes, well." He turned the page.

We continued looking at the pictures. There were a lot of the couple before they were married and then quite a few of the wedding party; it had been a large celebration. I continued turning the pages, and we came to the reception in the dark recesses of the Seelbach's Rathskeller. There I stopped. Horace Laroveneur stared out from the photograph taken ten years ago. He was seated at a table with Miriam and a young Brett and the man I took to be Brett and Gray's grandfather, plus a few other people I didn't recognize. Gray was not in the shot. The party was seated at a cloth-covered table beneath a heavy, tiled arch. Everyone gazed off camera toward, presumably, the happy couple who would have been just to the side of the balcony, against the north wall, if I correctly recalled the visit Gray and I had made to the room. In back of the guests and to either side, were other tables filled with people under equally baroque Rookwood tiles and arches, all caught in a moment, observing something off camera.

"Gray, turn up the light, would you please?" I said. There was something odd about the picture.

Gray sat back down after reversing the dimmer a bit more. "Do you see anything strange about this picture?" I said, pointing to it.

He bent over it and didn't say anything for a couple of minutes.

I couldn't put my finger on it but there was something bothersome about the shot.

"They're all looking at something," I said.

"Yeah, that must have been when Amelia cut the cake."

I couldn't put my finger on what was unsettling about the photo. Besides, of course, the presence of Horace, who now that I thought about him came more forcefully into focus concerning Brett's death.

"Do you know where Horace was the night Brett was attacked?" I said.

Gray gave me a glance. "Julia . . . ."

"No, I'm not accusing him. I'm simply wondering,"

"Well, you can stop wondering. He and Miriam are in Montreal for the week."

Well, I thought, he still could have masterminded it. Just because he didn't wield the weapon doesn't mean he wasn't involved. I held my tongue; that logic the police could apply to more than one person.

"Can I keep this photo for a little while?" I said. "I just want to study it."

Gray shrugged. "Sure."

A while later he asked me if I wanted to drive back

to the guest cottage or stay the night at his house. "The guest room upstairs is made up. But you wouldn't have any clean clothes."

I thought about the computer and opted to stay, asking to borrow a Brookfield Stud polo shirt from Gray for tomorrow.

"That works," he said.

I had set the alarm in the guest room and awoke without effort at 3:30. The farm work began at dawn so everyone involved was well-used to retiring and rising early. I assumed Gray would be sound asleep from long habit, but I would still need to be cautious; his was an unfamiliar house, and his bedroom was just off the study.

I made my way down the curving stairs without mishap. Fortunately, there was more than a sliver of moon, and with the numerous windows, the living room, hallway, and study were not completely dark. I stole over to the computer, very thankful that the door to Gray's suite was securely closed; at least I'd have a moment's notice should he wake.

I tapped the mouse and the screen came alive. First I called up my email in-box and docked it at the base of the screen. Then I set to work, employing every nefarious trick taught me by Gwyneth.

The Brookfield website was an obvious icon and when opened, had the password already plugged in; I easily shot through the behind-the-scenes portions but found nothing of interest. I'd already seen the stallion bookings in Gray's office at Brookfield; the only other thing listed there were simulated breedings—there was a cache of proposals made during the year for or from broodmare owners.

I sat back and thought for a moment. I recalled Horace had a lot of broodmares and some stallion interests. I clicked the icon for the broodmares on the farm; they were divided into those living there and those shipped in. I scrolled down each list looking for anything out of the ordinary. Every mare on the farm had a history, so when I found one owned by Horace, I read the background.

Nothing.

Next I looked again at the stallions. Here, unlike on the farm's computer in Gray's office, each stallion had financials and ownership history links. I investigated the likely suspects and stopped when I came to Aury. When Gwyneth had looked over Horace's finances, she'd found he had a big stake in that horse—the one Gray felt was about to "break out," as he put it. I read up on Aury and was suitably impressed; his breeding did suggest his "babies" would do well. I investigated Chance and Ataway Raj and a few others and saw that Horace had at least some participation in more than a few stallions via the syndicate. This was news. My impression was that his major interest had been on the broodmare side. I filed this information away; you never know what's going to be of use down the road.

I searched the desktop for other, more interesting folders or site icons. Nothing popped out at me. I went online directly and pulled down the URL bar to see what sites Gray had last visited. South African Racing and Dubai websites were listed as well as Saratoga, Ashford Stud, and Gainsborough. I guess Gray had been keeping up with the latest industry news, both here and abroad. I clicked on his email and was sent directly back to the Brookfield site, only this time a password was required. I thought a moment, and entered, "Prospector" with no result, then "Stallion" with no luck, and a few other brainstorms I had, but nothing worked. I wished I could call Gwyneth.

Next I accessed the computer's hidden history, which showed a longer list of websites visited. The same sorts of sites were listed there as on the pull-down menu with the addition of an A.G. Edwards address, an E-Trade address, and a few other investment firms. He'd also visited a Cozumel and Puerto Vallarta address.

I had begun to hit dead ends . . . and I was tired.

I yawned and closed my eyes for a moment. When I opened them, I was staring at the barrel end of a big, steel gray gun.

"What *the hell* are you doing?" said Gray with some fierceness. He didn't lower the gun.

I had my hand on the mouse so I clicked the base of the screen as I said, "I couldn't sleep." I yawned again to suggest my utter exhaustion. "I was just checking my email." When my eyes met his, I held them. "I'm missing my classes Tuesday. Remember?"

Gray lowered his gun. "Jesus, Julia. I could have killed you."

He sat down next to me and set the gun on the desk beside the computer. I eyed it with some concern. He put his arm along the back of the chair I was sitting in.

"I heard something out here, and . . . *Jesus,* Julia," he said again. "Couldn't this wait until the morning? I really could have killed you." He did seem upset about it.

I smiled, ruefully, I hoped. "Sorry."

"You're taking Brett's death pretty hard, aren't you." It was a statement, not a question.

He was correct. "I guess I am."

Gray closed his eyes and took a deep breath; he was tired, I could tell.

"Yeah . . . me, too."

I wanted to confess right then and there, but I didn't have enough hard evidence on Horace, and I knew Gray would revert to that furious voice he'd used just moments ago—one I didn't need to hear again.

The moonlight filtered in and pooled silver on the desk, illuminating the gun. I couldn't take my eyes of it. It was a large gun.

"Listen," said Gray, "I really can't afford to stay up. I'd like to keep you company but I need to work in the morning." He stood and picked up his gun. "Do you think you can get back to bed or should I make you some . . . milk?" He smiled tiredly.

"No, I'm fine. I'll head upstairs. I think I can sleep." It seemed Gray was either completely oblivious or he didn't really want to know what was right in front of his face.

I headed upstairs not knowing which it was.

I suppose it is a luxury of ownership not to have to be at the farm at the crack of dawn like everyone else if you'd been up at 3:45 in the morning. I came down to the kitchen for breakfast about 8:30 to find Gray dressed, shaved, and reading the paper, which made me feel like the slug I was.

"Sorry, you should have woken me," I said. "Go on to the farm if you need to. I'll get cleaned up and hang out here until eleven if you like."

He folded the paper and sipped his coffee at the bar. Sunlight streamed in through all the windows. "No, take your time. I've been up for a while and did some work on the computer, cleared my desk of a few things. I'm fine."

I wondered if he could tell what I'd actually been doing in the dead of night.

He rose and went around to the kitchen side of the bar. "How about some eggs?"

The thought of food first thing in the morning turns my stomach.

"Coffee would be fine." That's all I can do. Coffee, then maybe a run, then, possibly, something to eat. I have an odd metabolism.

"Actually, I'll just grab a cup and run back upstairs and dress," I said. I trotted up the stairs, gulping coffee, and jumped into the shower.

180

After a shower in which I lingered probably a tad too long, I toweled my hair, scrunched it, dressed in the beige polo with the Brookfield logo and my jeans and sneakers from the day before. I was circling down the stairs when I heard Gray on the phone. "God-*Damnit*. . . . No, I know. But *Jesus*. Call Tim." He slammed down the phone. "God-Damnit," he said again forcefully.

"What happened?" I said, coming to the side of the bar.

He was nearly purple-faced. "Aury."

My heart sank.

"God-*Damnit*." Gray put his hands on his hips and walked in a circle around the black granite island in the kitchen. I didn't say anything; he was definitely on the edge.

"He covered a God-damned mare, they took him back to his stall and he fell down dead."

"Oh, Gray."

"He was a God-damned good stallion. Maybe a great stallion. God . . ." He threw his hands out in front of him. "*Damnit*."

"Come on," he said, "I have to get over there."

We left. I didn't say a word the whole way.

When we arrived, Horace was in the parking lot waiting for Gray. I thought he was in Montreal. I looked at Gray but didn't mention it. Horace looked serious but I wouldn't say sadness had anything to do with it. Gray got out of the Navigator and strode over to him and Horace took his hand. They shook and walked into the office. I opened the door, got out, and followed them in.

I confess I was livid. If Horace had come anywhere near me, I think I might have strangled him then and there.

Tim was talking to Marcy and Lillian, and I joined them. Lillian saw Gray speaking with Horace, and when she turned to me, she looked old suddenly, her eyes full of sorrow. I knew what she was thinking: this was love's loss, not business. I looked at Tim questioningly, and he followed me over to the coffee pot. He got right to the point.

"With insulin," he said, "if it's artificial, if somebody injected Aury, it will show up in the eye."

I started to speak but Tim went on.

"This one's going to the lab," he said and angrily walked into Gray's office.

They had already closed Gray's office door, so I went to Marcy. "Sometimes it happens," she said. "Happened to three of Claiborne's best stallions— Buckpasser, Herbager, Princequillo. All of 'em had heart attacks in the breeding shed. Princequillo didn't die for a month but it happens."

Lillian stood close, rubbing the back of her neck with one hand, her other on her hip, looking at the floor, nodding. She remembered some of those horses, I realized. Remembered and mourned them.

No, I thought. This did not feel right by any stretch of the imagination. Foals, then Brett, now Aury. No way this was business as usual.

I gave Lillian a warm, embracing hug as best I could, given my anger, and headed out the door and up to the guest cottage.

Which had been ransacked.

I rushed to the mahogany table where my computer and notes and books had been neatly arranged the day before. Now there was chaos, as if someone had taken two hands and swirled it all into a fine mess.

I looked around. Just as with Brett's living room, the couches were stripped, and I knew if I went into the bedroom the mattress would be off the bed and my clothes in a heap.

I also knew what the intruder had been after. I pulled my purse close. Like Brett, I hadn't felt comfortable leaving the postcard behind so I'd tucked it into my purse before leaving for Gray's house.

Rather than feeling violated, as seems always to be the case with break-ins of this nature, I felt a surge of . . . elation. This ransacking was proof positive that Brett's intuitions had been correct; why else search my research on his family? I felt this break-in confirmed Brett had been killed because of the contents of that box, and that the postcard I had contained some important clue that I just hadn't been quite able to figure out yet. I pulled out the postcard and re-read the sentence that still sounded odd to my ears: "quiet, with sweet drinks, happy people, and fair weather. Truly beautiful."

Why did the words haunt me so?

I felt somewhat smug that the intruder had found nothing of value in my notes or on my computer, because there wasn't anything there to find. Unless the person was an English professor and classics librarian, my Filson research and my notes on the Keats correspondence would be meaningless to him . . . or her.

Finally it was all beginning to make sense to me.

I would have bet my life that Aury had been insured for a whole lot of money. And a major beneficiary of that money was Horace, because Horace had the major percentage of that stallion.

Gray had said you could kill a foal or a horse in untraceable ways.

Well, I didn't need proof that someone associated with this farm was behind all this. Now I knew who that was, without question. I'd get my own proof in due time.

21

After reporting the break-in and answering the dozen questions the police detective had for me, I was left to clean up the mess, pack my things, and head home. The police were no closer to solving Brett's murder. They felt the ransacking of my belongings was an ominous note, but I knew it meant that Brett's murderer was no closer to finding the Keats treasure than I was.

I sat at the dining table, gathering my notes, books, and computer, and felt a surge of mixed emotions. On the one hand, the situation was reaching a sort of critical mass, and I sensed that very soon, if I just kept putting one foot in front of the other, I would have a clarity that I did not, at present, possess. At the same time, I felt anger about Brett's premature death mixed with the fondness I'd developed for him.

I pulled out the wedding reception picture to take one more look at the fifteen-year-old Brett seated next to the grandfather he'd been so sure was not a dissolute character. His hair was unruly, just as it had been the first day I'd met him, and he had the same relaxed smile I'd seen in between his anxious moments. Miriam and Horace sat to one side of Brett and his grandfather, and around them other guests looked on in happy anticipation as the newlyweds, somewhere off camera to their right, cut the cake. Above the guests, lurking on the heavy arches, Rookwood pelicans stared down at the celebration like so many expressionless gargoyles.

Then I noticed what was odd about the photo. It was the line of sight of the guests. Everyone's eyes were trained off camera to the right: Brett's, the Laroveneurs, the guests at the tables to their right and in back of them. Everyone except Brett's grandfather, the person who posed such a mystery to his family. He was what bothered me; his angle of sight disrupted the otherwise uniform direction of vision. He was looking elsewhere, slightly left of the cake festivities and upward.

What was he staring at?

I sorted through the papers in front of me to see if I had any information about that room. I didn't. Gray had taken me down there following his syndicate meeting to share something about his family so there wasn't a reason for me to record any notes about the room.

I tried to recollect what it looked like, what was against that far wall that Brett's grandfather might be looking at. Of course, I realized the fact that he looked elsewhere could mean absolutely nothing. Maybe an interesting painting hung on that wall and he was bored. Maybe he was lost in thought about something unrelated to the events around him. Maybe . . . well, there were a million maybes. Still, something tugged at me. When I probed it, what came to mind was not that wall, it was the pelicans.

The postcard I had from Brett's cigar box also had a pelican. Brett's grandfather had left him the contents of that box and presumably everything in it was a clue, if Brett's intuition had been correct. As I had already agreed it was.

I fished it back out of my purse, only this time I

didn't read the message; I looked at the photograph of the Florida pelican. I felt sure the picture was Brett's grandfather's attempt to direct attention to the Rathskeller.

I flipped the card over and again read:

> *This is the most beautiful place. And so quiet, with sweet drinks, happy people, and fair weather. Truly beautiful—what else do we need?*

I looked up, and my eye fell on the *Norton*, open to "Ode on a Grecian Urn," and I read the first line:

> *"Thou still unravished bride of quietness."*

A variation of the word "quietness" also appeared in the sentence on the postcard. What if Brett's grandfather had been looking in a different direction in the wedding photograph—away from the festivities—because he couldn't help himself? What if he was mesmerized by something pertinent to the puzzle in front of me?

I continued reading Keats' poem. The first line in the second stanza reads:

> *"Heard melodies are sweet, but those unheard"*

There the word "sweet" occurs on the postcard, too. I jumped to the first line of the third stanza:

> *"Ah, happy, happy boughs! that cannot shed"*

I felt a surge of adrenalin. The postcard sentence had haunted me for a reason. I'd been reading and studying "Ode on a Grecian Urn" since high school; something in my subconscious mind had recognized this phrasing. So far, one word from the first line of each stanza appeared in the postcard sentence.

It seemed odd that Brett's grandfather would be that obscure if he was, in fact, referring to the famous poem. Who but an English scholar would be able to figure out his phrasing came from the ode? Certainly not Brett. But, I reasoned, perhaps his friend Jacoby, to whom the postcard was addressed, was one of those well-read gentlemen of the period and Brett's grandfather was simply trying to cover his bases in case something untimely happened to him.

As it had to Brett, I reminded myself.

Maybe this postcard was just one of the clues the grandfather had left those around him; it just happened to be the only one that survived. Perhaps others were left for relatives, but just as with the dubious care George Keats' letters were given by Georgiana's second husband, they were lost or discarded. It seemed logical that Brett's grandfather would assume all Keats descendants would be familiar with the poems of their famous relative and so might puzzle out references to them, such as on the postcard. I mean we're talking about John Keats, not some obscure 13th century Persian poet. Everyone read Keats, not just English scholars. Descendants of the famous writer would surely have read the work more closely than most.

Then I thought about the other phrasing on the postcard. What if "This. . . place" didn't mean Florida, where Brett's grandfather had been vacationing at the time this card had been written? What if "this place" meant the Seelbach, where he lived? What if Brett's grandfather was signaling to Jacoby, his friend, and later to Brett—calling attention to something at the Seelbach?

The fourth stanza begins:

"Who are these coming to the sacrifice?"

And the fifth and last:

"O Attic shape! Fair attitude! with brede"

"Fair" was also written on the postcard.

Brett's grandfather had used nearly every word from each stanza's first line as a reference to this poem. The significance of the words "truly beautiful" and "what else do we need?" also suddenly became clear: the last lines of the ode reads:

Beauty is truth, truth beauty,—that is all
Ye know on earth, and all ye need to know.

What else do we need? There was no doubt in my mind.

Not only had Brett's grandfather left these clues on the postcard; quite possibly, the man had unwittingly provided insurance. In the wedding photo, Brett's grandfather could have unconsciously been staring at an additional clue to this intricate and frustrating puzzle. After all, I reasoned, he had lived at the Seelbach for decades, and he'd not had visible means of support. Maybe he had found George's treasure. Maybe what he stared at in that photograph could help me unravel what had become an enigmatic dilemma. Or perhaps in the photo, he was staring at the treasure itself.

He might also simply be musing about something lost to history, I realized. But which was it?

I sat in the midst of a ransacked room and considered my options. Gwyneth was pinch hitting for me; she makes a stupendous guest lecturer, and my students always love her brilliance, not to mention her dry humor.

Albert adored being with her, and the feeling was mutual. I had nothing to do that couldn't be postponed at the library, and Gray was likely preoccupied with insurance issues, with possibly some police work thrown in. Lillian could fend for herself; she'd been doing it quite successfully without me for years.

The Seelbach was a little over an hour away, and I could be there by eleven-thirty or noon at the latest. I should have straightened up before leaving.

But I didn't.

I called Gwyneth to again thank her for covering for me. She said, "No, problem, you owe me." I hauled my computer, my purse, and a yellow pad of paper to the car and off I went.

I parked in the back and entered the Seelbach from the rear, crossing through the lobby and down the circular stairs to the lower level. Ahead, down the hall, I saw that the room was being readied for a banquet; waiters and waitresses in street clothes carried tablecloths and silver into the room. I joined them, thinking this must have been the scene just prior to the wedding reception pictured in the photograph in my purse. Consulting it as I walked through the Rathskeller, I tried to position myself in the room about where Brett and his grandfather had been sitting. Though a few people smiled at me, no one took notice of my presence beyond that.

I stood between two pillars and looked towards the far wall. To the left was the entranceway. To the right of that were two arched Rookwood pottery plaques, floor to ceiling in height, depicting Bavarian houses and flowering trees. The first archway contained what appeared to be two family crests. The next one was more elaborate; at the top was a stained glass window, below that a fretwork balcony, and below that two series of panels inset with alternating

189

green and blue openwork tilings. To the right of this was a heavy overhead archway lined with pelicans, beneath which, I thought the cake-cutting ceremony had likely taken place.

I glanced at the picture, positioning myself where the Laroveneurs and Brett would have been sitting. Yes, they all seemed to be looking in the direction of a place just beneath the pelicans to the right. I tried to line my sight with where Brett's grandfather seemed to be looking. To the left and up.

I was staring at the balcony below the stained glass windows. I moved closer. The wood was dark and it seemed familiar to me. I stared at it as around me the waitresses and waiters snapped white tablecloths and laid silver. After a few moments a picture formed in my thought; the wood splinter in Brett's box—its stain seemed to closely match the color before me. I stepped closer, and my inspection showed the two to be extremely similar, if my recollection of the one in Brett's cigar box held true.

I glanced down to the Rookwood panels below the balcony. The color of the blue tiles might have been similar to the rubble in Brett's box, but I couldn't be sure since I didn't have it at hand. I recalled that both Jacoby and Brett's grandfather had lived at the hotel during the construction of this room; it had been remodeled around the year 1907. Brett's grandfather would have had access to the Rathskeller during its construction and could easily have gathered the splinter and tiling fragments as the construction progressed.

Looking up again at the balcony, I noticed that the stained-glass window was actually two windows that closed seamlessly. I peered upward, inspecting the balcony with my hands; it was attached to the wall, so it could have been added at a date separate from the installation of the walls themselves.

190

I walked back a few paces. One of the waiters asked if I needed some help. I smiled and said I was fine, suspecting he assumed I was part of the booking he was setting up for.

The stained glass was lit from behind. I wondered if I could open the windows from wherever the lighting originated. The doorway out of the Rathskeller revealed an office up a few steps to the right. It was open, so I entered and found it to be empty but for a plethora of packed boxes stacked against the wall; it appeared the occupants had already moved to new quarters. The window I was looking for was just to my right, complete with two wrought iron window levers; the windows could be opened from there. I pressed the levers and swung open the windows to look out into the Rathskeller from above the balcony. Below me the wait staff continued to move through the room setting up for a party. No one glanced up.

Then I looked down onto the top of the balcony and noticed a dark, slitted opening between the balcony itself and the tiling, as if the wood had warped slightly or had been man-handled to force a slim repository. It was too dark to see inside the opening, and I had no flashlight. I bent out the window, squinting to see into the darkness just below, but I couldn't make out a thing. I didn't want to put my hand into that crevice, but I had to either put aside my aversion to whatever might be crawling around in there or risk losing what Brett's grandfather might have secreted there.

I looked away and stuck my hand down the dark opening, feeling what I hoped was the dust of years and not spider webs.

My fingertips hit something. I glanced into the room quickly to see if anyone was observing me. No one had looked my way. I bent and again peered into the opening, letting my hand play along what I'd found. It felt like a long, narrow piece of old, dry leather with a flat knob of some sort on one end, wedged into place. I grasped it and pulled up a leather portfolio about twenty inches tall, hand-sewn completely shut. Attached to one side was a very long, slim circular leather casing that measured about three feet in length, sewed in a hinged fashion to the leather portfolio.

I can't say my pulse raced. I was too dumbstruck for that. I withdrew into the office, closed and latched the window. My first instinct was to get the thing opened as quickly as I could, but I had nothing to cut with, and I wasn't sure I should. I inspected the dark brown leather closure and saw that the leather used to close the portfolio, or bag, was brittle. I sat down and carefully unwound then peeled off the leather cord binding. As I did that, the tubular portion nearly fell completely away so brittle was the leather used to bind it to the portfolio. I set down the thin receptacle gently and peeked inside the circular tube. There were rolled thickened papers; I counted seven, but I couldn't be sure how many were in there. I set it aside and picked up the portfolio.

I put my fingers gently into the slim opening and pulled out a thick, discolored sheet of paper on which was written in scrolling hand "Ode on a Grecian Urn." There followed the complete poem, hand-written in its original form, signed by the author, John Keats.

I had in my hand the original poem I'd been certain had once been in the possession of George Keats. It was worth a fortune, and I could do nothing but stare at it. I was unable even to read it.

22

I did the right thing. I went to the Horschow, where I placed the manuscript and what I assumed were "sketches" and hand-colored engravings by John J. Audubon into the hands of our astonished curator. I also mentioned that he should call the Seelbach to report the finding, knowing full well that eventually Lillian and Gray, among others of the Keats family, would come to claim them. However, I reasoned, before that eventuality at least the document, painted "sketches," and engravings would be properly cared for and their conservation seen to by professionals. I fervently hoped I would not be arrested for stealing them, but I have to say I would have placed the findings in the proper hands if I'd had the whole thing to do again.

At the Horschow, the poem would be authenticated, kept in a climate-controlled environment, and otherwise well looked after until claimed and, most likely, auctioned to the highest bidder. Ditto with the artwork by Audubon.

However, turning them all over, I admit, I did not do right away.

I first wanted to have them all to myself, just for the short time it took to have what I'd found truly sink in.

Lillian's "sketch," I knew, would be authenticated. The reason I felt so sure was that the first engraving I withdrew from the protective tubing was a full-blown rendering of the swans she had given me only a short time before but which seemed like years ago. So our university curator had been correct; Audubon had followed his usual habit and turned Lillian's lovely "sketch" into a vivid, beautiful, fully-hand-colored engraving. There were others, too, and I knew the 1827 edition of *The Birds of America* which had so impressed George Keats would be supplemented by what I had in my possession. George, I thought, dear George, had preserved these for his wife and family, knowing they'd be worth something to them but not knowing into whose hands they would eventually fall.

I was happy they were mine.

It was the ode that truly touched my heart, not only because of its meaning—that finally art outlasts mortality (a theme the very presence of the poem in my hands verified)—but because a man I'd come to respect and admire had held this very sheet. Touching it moved me with the sort of reverence most people feel in church.

The ode itself was of rare value, but to me the reverse side was also of great interest. It contained sketches of four pillars very much like the ones I'd recalled from Brett's cigar box, plus the phrase: *For Isabelle,* which appeared to be written in the same hand as George's journal. On one pillar was drawn a crude urn, on the second a young woman and man. The third and fourth showed a seated figure with a lute and an altar laid with flowers. The urn, of course, was intriguing because of George's journal comment.

The series of sketches was more developed and detailed than the ones in Brett's cigar box, but they were similar enough to have represented the same structure. And of course the dedication was intriguing; I wondered when they had been drawn; often, I knew, young ladies of the era were married beneath constructed pergolas in their families' gardens. I wondered if this sketch reflected George's early plans for his ill-fated daughter's wedding. Certainly the date of the ode on the reverse side would support that; George would have been in possession of his brother's famous poem long before Isabelle neared marital age. The depictions might suggest a celebration and marriage: a couple, a marital urn, music, and an altar.

I photocopied both sides and enlarged images of the sketches.

The day of the discovery I had called Gray from the Seelbach with the news and to hear if there was any additional information that might help me understand Brett's murder. To his credit, though immersed in insurance and syndicate dealings associated with Aury, he seemed excited to hear of the find; he'd tell Lillian right away about the Audubon pieces. I didn't mention the drawings on the back of the ode.

One day soon, I knew, I'd have to turn over the manuscript and artwork to the Horschow, and after enduring question after question at the library about "my" manuscript and "my" Audubon pieces, I'd return to my home bereft of tangible evidence that George Keats had ever been a part of my life.

But not just yet.

Late in the day, towards the end of that week, I settled in for some coffee and a serious bit of detective work back at my apartment. Albert had plopped down at the door, covering the entranceway completely with his big, white, prone body. True to her word, Gwyneth had placed her findings about Horace in my office behind the terra cotta Rachel—why she felt secrecy was requisite eluded me; sometimes I think Gwyneth reads too many murder mysteries. The accounts about Horace showed nothing I

195

hadn't concluded from Gwyneth's phone call.

I felt no closer to solving the rest of the Keats riddle than I had earlier in the week but was determined to piece it together if that was at all possible. First, for Brett. Secondly, because I needed to find definitive proof of Gray's innocence and who, in fact, had murdered Brett.

I moved the coffee table and on the rug I set out everything related to Brett, George's journal, and Gray; I separated and straightened each piece so I could see it all clearly in one glance. Armed with my yellow pad and fine-point pen, I got down on the floor with all the papers. First there was the postcard: on one side, a pelican; on the other side the words "quiet, sweet, happy, and fair," which I finally understood.

Second: I had listed the contents of Brett's box on a single sheet of paper since I no longer had access to it: dark brown wood splinter circled in old lace; bluish powder with some rubble in the same color; very old sketched drawings of columns or pillars; the old paper scrap in Samuel Keats' hand reading, "The secret is safe with Isabelle." I thought over the phrase: Did the secret he referred to have to do with Isabelle's death? Was she, in fact, murdered—was that the secret? Was there evidence somewhere that she had committed suicide as some at the time suspected? Perhaps the secret referred to the money George had left for his family. I had so many questions about the contents of Brett's cigar box, my mind fairly whirled. Why did the sketches of the pillars appear here and on the back of John Keats' manuscript? Had George drawn both, or were they done by someone else, and to what purpose?

Third: There was a pile of financial reports having to do with Horace Laroveneur and his wife Miriam. Horace was close to broke and Miriam had substantial assets. I wondered if they had a prenuptial agreement; perhaps that's why Horace remained with Miriam. But why on earth would anyone remain married to Horace?

Fourth: George Keats' journal. I allowed it to remain closed due to its deteriorating condition, but on top of it I'd placed a paper with the typed words: December 3, George exhorts Samuel, says he's saved a "rich treasure" and that he, Samuel, must assume responsibility for the family.

Other than the sketches and John's original poem, I had not come across any urn in any other dealings—not in conversation with Brett, not in the cigar box, not in my Filson research, or in the Keats correspondence.

I shuffled through my photocopies, and found the sketch of the urn on the back of the original ode. I placed this beside the journal. Something niggled at my thought about the urn but hard as I tried, it would not clarify itself.

Fifth: The photograph of the Rathskeller reception. Though I had solved its riddle it might still have some relevance so I laid it out with the rest of the artifacts.

Sixth: I had opened my copy of the *Norton Anthology of English Literature*, Vol. 1 to "Ode on a Grecian Urn."

There, I thought. The answer to George and Samuel and Brett's mystery was right in front of me. For the life of me, though, I couldn't see it.

I sat a while staring at the neatly arranged clues. If I could just clear my thoughts. Sometimes interesting ideas float to the surface when my mind is quiet.

I got up and made a fire.

I went to the kitchen and poured a glass of cranberry juice and got a dog biscuit for Albert.

I gave the treat to Albert, who sniffed then gobbled it, went back to the living room, set down my glass, picked up my pad, and stared at the neatly arranged clues.

This was not working. I thought maybe moving the clues might joggle my mind a bit. I'd place clues that had any relationship whatsoever next to each other and see what happened. I put the photograph of the wedding next to the financial reports on Horace and his wife; both people were in the photograph. Below that, I put the list of what had been in Brett's cigar box next to George Keats' journal. Next to that I placed the photocopy of the sketch on the back of the ode. I put the postcard next to the photograph of the wedding reception because Brett's grandfather was in the photo and had lived at the Seelbach. Between the two sets of clues, I placed the poem, "Ode on a Grecian Urn."

I stood up, so I could see the new arrangement from a different vantage point. My slight anal-retentive streak kicked in as I stood up; I'd nudged the Laroveneur's financial reports out of strict alignment, so I bent down to straighten them at the corners and noticed something on one of the papers sticking out beneath Horace's reports.

I pulled out the first of Miriam's financial records. "Oh my God," I whispered, looking at it, aware that only Gwyneth had studied these pages. I'd seen Horace's financial records but not Miriam's. I looked up at the mirror above the fireplace and saw myself standing there, literally open-mouthed.

As the significance of what I had glimpsed began to dawn on me, I realized that had I not left the interpretation of the Laroveneur's financial condition to Gwyneth, I might have noticed this detail. If I had, Brett might still be alive. "Oh my God," I said again and stared down at the page in my hand. It had been here all along.

I set Horace's pages neatly in a pile to the side and picked up the remaining ones reporting on Miriam's holdings.

I looked more closely at her bank statements, investment accounts, dispersals, partnerships, and syndicate participations and said a silent prayer to the IT God Gwyneth worships.

The entire situation came to me with complete clarity as if the tumblers in a safe had fallen into place. I saw that none of this had ever been about George Keats or Brett, or the ode, or the hidden riches. That had all been a decoy. I stared at the top of the financial report I held in my hand, and I knew precisely what she had done, how she had done it, and how the last tumbler in her plan was about to fall into place.

My first impulse was to call Gray.

I really hoped it was the right thing to do.

He picked up on the third ring, and I explained to him what I'd just discovered. I asked him if the Laroveneurs were in town and where they lived. He insisted, though wearily, on accompanying me to their house and wouldn't hear of me confronting Miriam alone. I was to drive to Brookfield the next day, meet him in the office, and we'd go over together. I said this had to be done immediately and that I'd be there in an hour and a half, then hurried to change my clothes and get on the road.

I called Gwyneth to inquire about any additional material she'd discovered about Horace; I had to know everything I could possibly know before getting to Brookfield. I needed one little edge if I hoped to prevent more murders.

I got Gwyneth's voicemail and left a message, asking her to look in on Albert. I patted his head on the way out, and he rolled his eyes at me, sighing. The dog has the patience of Job.

By the time I'd pulled into the Brookfield office driveway, it was about 6:15. Marcy, the accountant, the breeding consultant, and the other staff were gone. I was thinking that I should probably have called the detectives who'd investigated Brett's murder to meet us at the office; I'd brought the financial records with me, illegally obtained though they were. Occupied with these thoughts, I was not prepared when I opened the door to see Gray, Horace, and Miriam sitting together in the outer office.

Gray spoke first. "Julia," he said.

Horace snickered.

"I thought if we just sat down together and talked this through, you'd see . . ." Gray trailed off once he saw my expression.

Is this man insane was the thought that flitted through my mind.

I looked at Miriam, who seemed as remote and unreadable as she had that evening in the Seelbach's Oakroom. She smiled, slightly.

I wasn't quite sure what to do. I understood everything that had occurred—why it had happened and how it had happened. But I had not prepared myself for this confrontation, and it was doubly disturbing to think that Gray had called in the Laroveneurs.

What the hell was I going to do now?

It didn't matter what I had figured out, I still had to prove it. I stood there obviously stunned and began to worry about where Miriam's relative might be. I had assumed Chaney went by his first name and, for the briefest moment, again, chastised myself for not looking at the financial records. It wasn't until I did look at Miriam's disbursements that I understood his full name was William Chaney, and that he was either Miriam Chaney Laroveneur's brother or uncle.

I glanced at the clock: 6:20. They were turning out the stallions at 7:00, and there would be people about then, possibly Chaney would be among them. If Gray had called the Laroveneurs just after speaking to me, Miriam would have had plenty of time to get in touch with him. I didn't like that; Will Chaney had already murdered one man, one stallion, and numerous foals. He'd have no trouble with me, I was sure of that.

I directed myself to Gray.

"I know you might not understand this, Gray, but all these things that have happened to your farm have nothing to do with Brett or his cigar box."

I hoped to God something I said would make sense to him.

"Really," said Horace. "And just what do you think has happened here, Miss Julia?" He paused. "Or would you rather have me call you *Ms.* Julia?" He grinned at Gray and then turned to Miriam.

I ignored him.

"Miriam," I said, taking the bull, literally, by the horns, "why don't you tell Gray something about your father? That's what this is all about, really. Isn't it?"

I was not sure what I was doing. There wasn't anyone here who could help me if things turned suddenly ugly.

Miriam simply put her large purse, which she'd held in her lap, on the table next to her and folded her empty hands in her lap. Her dark hair was swept into a long barrette in the back. She had on black Capri pants and a checkered blouse.

"My father?" she said. "Why ever do you want to know about him?"

Gray added, "What do you think has happened here, Julia?"

I did not want to sit down, and I wanted to stay near the door. How I wished I'd just called the police on the drive down.

"The foals? Aury? Do you think those were accidents?" I said to Gray.

Horace laughed out loud this time. "Julia, Julia . . . Your imagination has taken flight, darlin'. It most certainly has taken flight right off the planet."

At the same time, Gray said, "If you knew anything

about horse breeding, you'd know . . ." He shook his head, now angry at me. "You have insulted Horace and Miriam, and . . . "

I saw Miriam make a move for her purse.

Gray didn't notice it, being caught up in anger towards me, and Horace was enjoying my discomfort too much to be paying attention to much else.

Miriam drew a very large, steel-gray handgun from her purse. Quietly she said to me, "They generally do underestimate us."

Horace turned and went slack-faced; it took him a few seconds to be appropriately appalled at the appearance of the gun. His dismay, I thought, came more due to his "little woman" having gone rogue than because he thought he was in any danger. Gray was completely taken aback, and then his face registered a slowly dawning understanding; he looked at me and I didn't like the resignation shadowing his face.

At least his shock might result in some useful action. Finally.

"My God," he said softly. He looked at Miriam but didn't say anything.

Horace tried to stand but Miriam waved him back down calmly with the barrel of the gun. He sank back, meek as a puppy.

I stood where I was, stunned, my eyes focused on Miriam's gun; she appeared all too comfortable handling it.

"Julia has astutely asked about my father," Miriam said. She glanced at the clock. I was then sure she was waiting for Chaney.

"Is William Chaney your brother, or uncle?" I said.

"Uncle." She stood up. "My father's brother." She smiled again.

"Let's take a little walk." Miriam motioned us ahead of her, and we all walked into Gray's office. The blinds were
202

down but open slightly so you could see out into the stallion complex, though I doubted anyone could see in from that distance even if they were looking.

Miriam motioned Gray to the chair behind his desk and Horace and me to the chairs in front of it. She remained standing at the door.

"When you look at that wall, Gray, what do you see?" she said, still in sotto voice, still calm, still very much in charge. She directed his gaze to the wall across from him with the many stallions, racing shots, plaques, and awards.

"I see a success we all built together," he said tightly. "I see stallions going back to *before* your father was here. I see hard work, heartbreak, triumph . . . Perseverance."

I recalled Gray's Tesio quote of the night before.

"You know what I see?" she said, moving closer to the wall. She surveyed each picture. "I see my father turning into a monster." She turned to Gray. "That's what I see up there."

I understood what she meant probably better than Gray or Horace. The two of them were so much a part of the industry they didn't see the toll it takes on people. They didn't see the pressure having to produce a winner had on trainers or anyone else in the business. I saw it, at least a little. I saw it at Keeneland, on the tote board as the odds changed, as the purses came in. Your bet brought you nothing if your horse didn't place. I saw the welts on the "babies" hindquarters from the stick. I saw it in the trainers standing beside their mounts, maybe hitting them with an electrical shock when no one was looking. I'd overheard a 2-year-old's trainer say without expression that he wasn't sure his horse could finish the race he'd just entered him in.

I understood Miriam's rage.

"You think Brookfield prospered because of my father, don't you?" she said to Gray. "Did you ever consider what it did to Shorty? What your prosperity cost *him*?"

Horace brightened. "Miriam, darling. That's the game. You know it. I know it. Shorty knew it. He didn't do anything he didn't *know* he was doin'."

Gray intervened. "Shorty was a great trainer . . . He did things with horses I don't think anybody else on the planet could have done."

While this conversation was unfolding, I'd been keeping my eye on the stallion complex as best I could through the narrow blinds. If Richard was on turn-out, he'd be at the barn soon and visible from that window. If I could get to the window I might be able to signal him. If, I thought, if he got there.

Miriam interrupted Gray. "Do you know how my father died?"

I recalled Gray said he'd drifted into Mexico and no one had ever heard from him again.

Horace blustered something unintelligible.

I noticed someone moving out on the gravel in front of the stallion barn.

"He shot himself in the head," she said flatly, "right in front of me. I was eight years old and alone."

I thought it might be Richard. I hoped it was Richard.

I hoped it wasn't Chaney.

"Do you know what happens when you put a gun to your temple and pull the trigger?" She said this, moving over to Horace to put her big, glinting gun up to his temple. He sat shock still.

Miriam smiled quite easily at him. "If you had any idea how many times I have thought about this moment."

"Miriam," whispered Horace, pathetically pleading with her.

"First a large section of the skull on the other side blows upward and parts of the brain surge out in globs. I had blood and bits of flesh all over me." She turned to Gray and commented, "The amount of blood is astonishing."

She peered down at Horace. "But the worst part is, he didn't die." She looked around at us. "I wasn't sure what to do, as I said, I was eight." She seemed to be asking for our advice.

"He was on the floor, moaning, and half his head and his eye was gone. The rest of his head was a bloody pulp."

She motioned to us with the gun. "This was my father you understand. You knew him, Gray. "

Gray looked stricken. He put his head in his hands.

Miriam continued, her voice flat. "I just sat down in the blood. He kept moaning. It was his voice but his head was simply red pulp. So I held his hand."

She patted the gun barrel against Horace's temple. "Right here. Seems he would've done a better job of it. Knowing him." She looked at Gray. "Wouldn't you say?"

She then seemed to come to her senses. "But of course, he did die. After some time."

Lillian had mentioned Miriam was taken to Ireland by her relatives. Now that made sense; they took her away from a horrifying, ugly scene. She'd returned like a moth to flame.

She withdrew the gun and looked at her watch. "But we won't do it like that tonight. A suicide would never do."

I saw comprehension dawn in Gray. "You tried to frame me for Brett's murder, didn't you?" I could see the enormity of the situation clarifying in his mind. "But that backfired . . . so now . . . this."

Miriam smiled.

In the split second it took her to look over at Gray to relish his dawning understanding, I rushed behind Miriam, pulled up on the blinds, and began to bang on the glass with my fist. I didn't care if I broke the glass. I just wanted to get

Richard's attention.

He glanced up and looked over our way. It *was* Richard. Whether he saw me or not wasn't clear.

Miriam laughed. Chaney, who'd just walked in behind me, also laughed. I stiffened when I heard it. He was not a person I fancied having to escape from twice. I slowly turned around.

"Good, you're here," said Miriam. "Please close the blinds," she said to me, and I did.

"Nice party," said Chaney. He leaned on the door jamb and folded his arms.

The light was beginning to fade as it got closer to 7:00, but outside there was still light enough to raise an alarm if I could just get there. I had visions of running, screaming and flailing my arms, into the stallion barn. I have no inhibitions when it comes to looking ridiculous.

Horace still did not comprehend the situation. "Miriam, you killed that young stallion groom?"

Chaney actually guffawed. Gray sat with his head down.

Still Horace persisted. "Miriam, you said you'd pay for Brookfield. You said you would fund the takeover. Why would you murder a groom?"

Finally I spoke up. "Because she hates you, idiot." I'd had enough of Horace.

At this, Miriam's smile widened. "Explain it to him."

I drew in a breath and thought to buy as much time as I could.

"She duped you into sabotaging the farm so Gray would have to sell out. She got you and Chaney to kill those foals so Gray would lose money. But that wasn't revenge enough. Her plan was to have you pressure Gray into selling and then have it look like Gray murdered you when he found out you'd sabotaged the farm." I paused. "She'd have

206

her revenge on Gray's family and get rid of you in the process."

Horace looked at Miriam in horror. "Why murder me?"

I wanted to repeat the idiot comment, but I just sighed and went on.

"Then Brett and his cigar box came along, and with Gray's financial difficulties, that seemed an easier Plan B. Everyone knew Brett had pestered Gray about the family "fortune," so Gray getting Brett out of the way seemed obvious—even the police thought it was true."

Chaney seemed to be getting antsy at the door. Miriam noticed, too. "Soon," she said in a soothing way to him.

"Continue," she said to me. She waved her big gun a bit.

"So they intimidated Brett, made him think Gray was after the money." I turned to Gray. "After all, it's as much yours as it was his. That's why Brett agreed to meet with you at the stallion barn—to confront you about what Chaney told him." I looked at Miriam. "It was Chaney who ran Brett off the road, wasn't it?" I didn't want to look at Chaney myself, but I heard him snicker. Miriam smiled calmly.

It had also been Chaney who called Brett that night in the foaling barn, I surmised. I remembered Brett's protest; the young groom didn't believe his cousin Gray could be the villain Chaney described to him.

"Gray meeting Brett at the stallion barn was perfect." I looked at Horace. "If for some reason pinning Brett's death on Gray didn't work—and finishing Brett off nearly didn't work due to Devil's lack of cooperation—there was still you waiting in the wings. The murder weapon would have turned up whether Devil cooperated or not. It implicated Gray. You were disposable at any time."

Gray looked bleak. Horace seemed to shrink into himself.

"Nicely done, Julia," said Miriam.

"I bet that's Gray's gun, isn't it Miriam?" I said. I had become bold with all the talking I'd done.

She bowed slightly. "Very nicely done."

We had a little mutual admiration society going.

Miriam seemed to be thinking things over. Where to dispose of us likely occupied her thought; I had thrown a wrench in the works, so she was having to improvise.

She spoke to Chaney. "Why don't you take Julia to visit Medes? He's a very nasty boy, maybe he wouldn't enjoy an unexpected visitor."

Chaney started to protest; they'd tried that one before and it hadn't worked out very well. "Don't worry. Devil took a shine to Brett. Medes doesn't share that weakness . . . and he doesn't know Julia." She motioned us out with her gun. "And Julia doesn't know a thing about horses."

So I was to be the stupid city girl wandering into a stallion's stall. The thought of fourteen hundred pounds coming down on me in the form of two hooves was fairly unpleasant.

"And we were getting along so well," I said to Miriam as Chaney hustled me into the outer office. I glanced at Gray, who started to rise. I shook my head at him.

I could still run.

We crossed the cemetery and passed by the fountain. It was now getting darker and as far as I could tell, there was no one around. I strained, hoping not to hear a gunshot coming from Gray's office.

We were heading towards the barn where the two stallions were housed, and we were still clearly in view out Gray's office window. Chaney had me in a death grip; if I got out of this, I'd be bruised for life.

He kept hold of me as he flicked the latch on the barn door and slid it open. Devil's stall was the first one on the right. Medes was housed on up the row. We entered the dimness and headed towards Medes' stall. Someone moved swiftly behind us, and came down hard on Chaney's arm with a breeding roll. He bent, letting go of me, and grabbed his arm. I was free.

Richard spun Chaney around and punched him in the jaw. Richard's upper body was a formidable weapon but Chaney put up his fists anyway. Devil and the other stallions caught a whiff of fear and perhaps testosterone and began stomping in their stalls, sending out deep, ominous gutturals. Anxious big animals give off a tension of their own. The barn was suddenly charged with feral animosity.

I backed against the wall across from Medes' stall as Richard hit Chaney's face with a right cross and then a hard left to his stomach. Richard did not say a word but bent to his task in earnest. It was dim in the barn but enough light glowed from the overhead bulbs high in the topmost part of the barn to illumine Chaney's pained and swelling face as he staggered, grunting, against Medes' stall. Inside the stallion reared and protested the assault at his door.

Richard moved in and continued his blows. Chaney somehow unlatched Medes' stall door. I watched in horror as he slid it back and stepped quickly aside hoping Richard's forward thrusts would drive the South African inside beneath the rearing stallion's hooves. Instead Richard bounced sideways with Chaney and with a quick shove, pushed him over into Medes' stall and slammed the door.

I stood dumbstruck, horrified as the sounds of Medes coming down on Chaney occurred over and over. The horse was frenzied, but the only sound coming from

Chaney was a whoosh of air from his mouth then Medes' angry cries.

"Guess Medes got his due," said Richard, peering in the stall and speaking quietly to the stallion. Medes finally heard Richard and bounded back toward the slim window, less and less frenzied, calmed by Richard's voice. He danced back against the wall where he nodded his big head up and down, still protesting the now still intruder. Richard grabbed the stallion shank and opened the door. "Whoa, boy," he murmured, stepping around Chaney's form. "Come on boy, it's all over." His voice was soothing, and he soon led Medes out of the stall. The stallion puffed up and skittered into the passageway, spooked by me or perhaps a shadow.

"He's breathing . . . barely," said Richard, referring to Chaney. "He's a bad sort."

I didn't have time to call anyone for him, bad sort or not. I still had to get Gray out of his office.

I filled Richard in after he'd deposited Medes in another stall, and we circled around the office building intending to enter from the side door, an approach Miriam couldn't see.

I used Richard's cell to call 911 on the way up, but I didn't have time to really explain. I hoped they'd send the detective I'd named in addition to the ambulance.

We crept in the side door of the office building and walked the short hallway beside the stairs. Gray's office was just ahead on the right. I had not yet heard a gunshot, so I presumed Miriam was still setting up how to stage the murder of her husband so as to frame Gray.

As we approached I heard Miriam speaking. From the sound of her voice, her back was to the window and she faced the hallway. I was glad of that because it meant perhaps she had not seen the events in the stallion barn and we would have the element of surprise.

She seemed to be enjoying the discomfort she was causing Horace and Gray. "Move your chair to the right, Gray. Please," she said.

I heard Gray's large old chair roll a bit on the wood.

"Now, Horace you face Gray as if you are just having a nice conversation."

Here Horace moaned.

"Horace, you've done this a thousand times, don't pretend you don't know what I'm talking about."

She sounded studied, a parody of wifeliness, as if she was scolding Horace for putting his shoes on the good furniture.

I thought this might be the only time in her life that Miriam had been in a position of any significant authority. She was enjoying the last few minutes of what she'd worked so hard for so long to realize.

Richard and I could not rush into the office as things stood. If we did, one or both of us would be shot. I just hoped Miriam would take a few more moments to admire her work before shooting her husband. She kept talking to both of them, commenting about how pleased she'd be to have Horace dead. She made a point to use that word—dead. She did not soften the blow, so to speak, at all. I figured Horace would be shaking pretty much all over by now.

Suddenly a shadow was cast into the hallway. It had to be Miriam, and it was our only chance. She'd probably come around Horace to survey the look of things from the doorway. I leapt into the door and Richard was right behind me.

All hell broke loose. Gray dove over the desk towards Miriam as the gun went off in Horace's direction. Miriam fell heavily to the floor with me and Richard on top of her. Gray grabbed the gun from her hand, and I looked up to see Horace literally huddling next to the window. He

211

slumped down to the floor, and I wasn't sure if he'd been hit or not.

"Julia," said Gray. "Julia. . . Richard!" He couldn't get out much more than that as he hauled Miriam to her feet and deposited her in the chair in front of his desk, just moments ago occupied by Horace who remained crouched under the window, still staring blankly at his wife. Blood oozed on his shoulder.

"I'm hit," he whispered.

None of us knew exactly what to do, and for a moment we all just stood there like statues. Miriam had her head in her left hand, hiding her face, while her other fiddled with her hair; she was trying to catch the stray strands into the barrette at her neck.

Richard sat down in the chair against the wall keeping an eye on Miriam.

I suddenly heard a siren. I wondered if it had been in the air for some time. It sounded close, but I had just noticed it.

Gray held the gun on Miriam but looked steadily at me, not yet relaxing.

Horace whispered again, "I'm hit."

23

Gray Burke was as contrite as I would ever see him, I was quite sure of that.

"I can't be any sorrier than I am," he said, much later that evening at his house as we sank into the couch, both exhausted. Gray sat close to me, which felt for the first time, completely comfortable. He had already apologized many more times than was needed for not taking me seriously and for calling the Laroveneurs.

"Don't worry about it," I said, once again, immersed in my own guilt for not figuring the whole thing out sooner. I leaned forward and poured myself a little more wine.

Gray was having Glenlivet tonight. He wasn't much of a drinker but tonight he'd poured one for his nerves. He sipped it rather demurely, I thought, not at all like the owner of a potentially successful stud farm, given the race returns he'd picked up from the voice recorder when we'd finally arrived at his home.

"When your runners do well, everyone calls to congratulate you. When they run poorly, your phone never rings," he'd said.

Two of his fillies had won in graded stakes, and Aury's son, Lock 'N Load, placed third in the Wood Memorial. Gray hadn't quite had time to keep abreast of the racing, so he relished the voicemails recounting the victories.

"He won't *win* the Derby," Gray stressed in response to the three-year-old's performance, "but he'll have enough points to get in it now."

I thought that somewhere on the farm, Lillian must be resting a bit more peacefully now that her son was cleared, and home, and safe.

We settled back in comfort and watched the lighted fountain outside burble.

"It's a Zen thing," Gray said.

After a while he asked me how I had put it all together.

I was really very tired, and the wine was sort of giving me a one-two punch. The truth was, I didn't feel too much like sorting back through it all, so I just said, "I don't know . . . It all just sort of clicked into focus."

He nodded. He had no idea what I was talking about, but he got it that I was too tired to talk about it. We sat quietly for a time, and I felt greatly relieved to have it all over.

"I just wish I had figured out where the Keats money is," I said, finally. To have found George's money for Brett and Gray would have meant a lot to me. Not for the money itself. It wasn't that I didn't feel very grateful to have found the manuscript and the Audubon paintings; I was looking forward to their reception by the academic and art worlds. I just thought the money would actually have helped Brett, made his life different in very real ways. Had he lived . . . . It certainly would have helped Gray out of financial difficulties that still loomed large.

"What did you think about Miriam's comments about her father?" I said, trying to hold back my feelings of responsibility for Brett's murder. I twisted around to look at Gray in the candlelight. Miriam had been taken into custody, and Chaney had been hospitalized. Horace had ridden along in the ambulance.

214

Behind Gray, over the fireplace, his family was spot-lit, and I noticed for the first time that the most prevalent aspect of the portrait was not the people—the focus was on the horse.

"Well, I do understand where she was coming from. I knew Shorty, and I watched him go down." He took a sip of his drink and savored it a moment. "But a lot of guys train horses or ride horses . . ." He trailed off for a moment and then resumed, "or breed horses, for that matter, and they never get to the point Shorty did."

"So all those stories about "needle" horses, and jockeys eating tapeworms, and the alcohol abuse on the track . . . all that isn't true?"

"Oh no, it's true," said Gray quickly, "though of course jockeys don't eat tapeworms anymore. But sure, bad stuff goes on. I'm not saying it doesn't." He stretched out his legs, plunking them on the table, and drew me closer with his arm.

"And what about a horse like Secretariat?" I said, from my position under his shoulder.

"He was a great horse. Some say *the* greatest horse."

I had been reading about horse racing since I'd met Gray. Not that that was a surprise to him.

"Well, I read that he was a hard-pounding, really big horse . . ."

"Yes, he was. Big Red, that's what they called him." Gray leaned up and repositioned himself so he could see my face.

"And that after his racing was done and he went to stud . . . ."

"Stood at stud," Gray corrected me, sipping, and listening, and watching me.

"Well, he got laminitis. In all of his feet. And maybe that's from all that pounding."

Gray didn't say anything.

215

I had read about horses that were euthanized, like Secretariat; the news reports simply read that the stallion had "died." They didn't specify that the vet had actually killed the stallion.

The fountain looked a lot more peaceful than the atmosphere in the living room suddenly.

"Do you want to go sit out on the patio?" I said by way of apologizing a little.

"Let me ask you this," said Gray, pointing at me with his glass after thinking it over. "Let's say you're a really great athlete." He saw my skeptical look, and sat up on the sofa. "No, now just think about it. Let's say you're a . . . basketball player."

I know less about basketball than I do about horse racing and the fountain seemed very appealing to me, as did the guest room. Gray had gotten a second wind from somewhere.

"Now the thing you love to do most in the world is play basketball. But," and here he paused for effect. "But if you play basketball you may ruin your knees, and when you are forty, you may end up a cripple, or something."

I could see where he was going. "But with horses, it's not their choice. Some trainers may drug them, or beat them, or whatever."

"Well, that's right. *Some* trainers. Not all trainers. Not my dad, that's for sure—he fought against it his whole life. And not me." Gray paused.

"Look," he said, taking another tack, "some trainers over train their human athletes, too. Some take drugs, and sometimes a boxer bites the ear of somebody, and sometimes human athletes break down just like horses . . . oh hell. There is truth to the darker side of the 'game,'" said Gray, the last word leaving a bad taste in his mouth. "I'm not denying that. But there is beauty, too. I'll take you to see some of my other horses run. They're so beautiful,

216

"poetry in motion," is what my father used to call it. You can just tell they're born to do it. And they love doing it." He trailed off, thinking I wasn't getting it.

Actually, I was. This was what Lillian saw in Gray and in his father. This was the love she'd been trying to get me to see, too.

I saw it. But I was really tired.

Gray had a last comment, though. "And sometimes just when you think things are going all to hell, Lock 'N Load comes in third in the Wood. Who would have thought?"

24

I returned home to my "normal" life the following day and picked up the puzzle's pieces—literally—from my living room floor with more than slight reluctance. Albert was glad to see me. I brushed, and rubbed, and made over him for quite a while, as he deserved, then took him for a long walk in Eden Park. Both of us needed to stretch our legs and walk out the kinks.

Though I was happy the threat to Brookfield and Gray had been eliminated, and I was grateful to have contributed John Keats' original manuscript to the scholarly record, and new Audubon engravings to the world at large, I admit what I felt was a lingering and persistent sadness at Brett's death. He'd been terribly innocent with a reluctance to admit that grief could come to him. His belief in his grandfather's character, too, showed a blind spot for a man who obviously had been living off the Keats' money, and the secret of its whereabouts had died with him—except for, perhaps, clues that neither Brett nor I could figure out in time. My sadness, too, had to do with my feelings of responsibility: had I only been more diligent, had I only inspected the Laroveneur's financial records myself, I might have prevented Brett's murder.

Home from our walk, I sorted through the remains I'd earlier gathered up. I'd have to turn over George Keats' journal soon enough, likely within the week. I fingered its black cover, which was in need of conservation work. It would be good to have it in a conservator's hands; that's where it belonged rather than in mine. Still, I was reluctant to let it go; the secret riches it referenced remained hidden. But truthfully, a part of me was content with that.

The next day was one of those very rare, April days full of fair skies and blooming flowers, and all was especially shimmering after a hard rain the night before. On impulse I decided to drive down to Cave Hill cemetery where George Keats is buried and bid him a final goodbye. This was certainly a trip of impulse; Cave Hill is just on the outskirts of Louisville. I thought only momentarily about the three-hour drive ahead of me.

I put Albert in the small garden back of the apartments and set out over the river.

This was something I needed to do.

Nearly and hour and a half later, around twelve-thirty, I drove through the imposing gates of Cave Hill, the lovely garden cemetery opened in 1848. The grounds had been planted with trees and flowering shrubs at its inception, and now the meandering roadways wound through towering oaks, elms, and sycamores, beneath which dogwood, redbud, and graceful blooming cherry trees flowered in pink and white. I passed tall marble statues of angels, men on horseback, busts of military men and monuments in white marble or granite standing amid carved headstones. It was a serene, calming, spiritually restorative atmosphere just as the designers had intended.

I found my way up the hill to Plot 73, the Keatses', overlooking a still lake marked only by the inverted "V" trailing a white swan. As I got to the gravesite, a peacock strolled out from behind the mausoleum I at first assumed was dedicated to George Keats.

I was wrong about that. George's grave marker was a simple monument that rose over four feet above my head, made of worn gray stone with a two-word inscription near the top that read *George Keats*. The ivy-covered mausoleum was dedicated to Isabelle and bore her name on the outside and her birth and death dates, though the last were obscured by ivy covering most of the top and sides of the small building. Its arched doorway was closed and, I presumed, locked.

I was surprised to find the opposite was true. I opened the door and wandered in.

In the center was a beautiful white marble sculpture of a young girl in a reclining position atop a darkened casket rimmed by shining brass rails. Someone was still tending to the brass. Around Isabelle's remains stood four granite pillars supporting a low sloping slate roof; Isabelle rested in her own small, covered rotunda within the larger space inside the mausoleum. Others of the Keats family were buried outside, close to George, but here there rested only Isabelle as testament to the central place she'd held in the family. I wondered if Samuel had commissioned the mausoleum and constructed it according to the plans left him by his father.

My eye traveled to the pillars, carved just as George had sketched out over a hundred and fifty years ago. I understood immediately, of course, the significance of what I saw there. But what struck me most forcefully was that the structure and carvings on the pillars testified to the love Samuel had for both Isabelle and his father.

I suddenly knew where George's riches were hidden.

The pillar to my left, behind the resting Isabelle, was carved with an empty, gracefully curving urn. Empty, but for one tulip leaning against the side of the lip.

I did not move for quite a while. The enormity of how many in the Keats family had kept George's fortune a secret impacted me. I sorted through the relevant dates: Cave Hill Cemetery was built in 1848, seven years after George Keats died. George and Isabelle were both moved to this site on April 9, 1879, when Samuel was 54 years old. It was Samuel who had written on the scrap of paper in Brett's cigar box: *The secret is safe with Isabelle*. Samuel knew well that the treasure was with Isabelle because he was the only one who could have put it there.

I felt keenly that George's hopes for Samuel had, after all, been realized. Samuel had looked after the family. He had lived up to his responsibility. George's treasure had likely been originally housed in a real urn then buried, as had other family heirlooms of that era. And Samuel had eventually carried out George's wish for his daughter's burial site, as the father had sketched them on the back of John's precious manuscript. Samuel's act would certainly be a fitting tribute to George, a man I felt I had come to know well, a man whose immediate and subsequent offspring, it seemed, followed in his footsteps.

I walked toward the pillar and noted how intact it appeared, though I knew George's money—or silver, or jewels, or whatever he had chosen to leave for his family's safety—was housed in or around it. The single carved tulip pended from the urn's edge, directing my eye to the marble floor surrounding Isabelle's casket.

Then I saw it.

Just at the base of the casket was a series of wooden panels enclosing the base upon which the casket rested. I knelt and tapped them one by one. They each sounded solid, but for one, which rang hollow. I knew that behind that panel, guarded by the reclining child, was where Samuel, likely still in grief over her death, had secreted his father's fortune.

I sat on the marble tiles. I thought over the impact of opening the panels. Certainly they had been opened before; from my vantage point, closer inspection revealed the slight scars resulting from previous entries and I was sure it was Brett's grandfather who had periodically visited his source of income. However, to reveal what I'd found to the public would expose the rest of the mausoleum to intense scrutiny. Isabelle's casket would certainly be opened and inspected. The inside of the monument would be searched inch by inch and I couldn't predict what damage might be done in such an inspection. The graves outside might be opened, the bodies exhumed. Who knows how many people would tramp through, disturbing the serenity in which the family had rested for over a century.

Enough damage had already been done, and I shared responsibility in more than a little of it.

I straightened and looked into Isabelle's cold white face.

Her secret would be safe with me.

Epilogue

It took a week for me to work through what seemed to make poetic, but not necessarily practical sense, and tell Gray about my find. We both met with Lillian, and the three of us decided to empty the cache Samuel had so long ago secreted in Isabelle's tomb. All of us were interested to see what George had considered important enough to preserve, and we were not disappointed.

I will include a partial list of the contents beneath a reclining Isabelle but preface it by mentioning that upon public release of our findings the predictable meetings with lawyers, extended family, etc., etc., ensued. It was agreed upon by all that the original documents relating to the poems of John Keats would be donated to the Houghton Library at Harvard. This collection is quite extensive and includes original poems in John's hand ("Lamia" as well as all the odes, among others) as well as copies George had made during his 1820 voyage to England. Included in the cache was also correspondence thought lost or suppressed by Georgiana's second husband John Jeffrey, between John and George from the year George emigrated through John's last tour of Italy.

All parties also agreed that the remaining artifacts

were to be housed at The Kentucky Historical Society and that Lillian Burke, much to her delight, would curate what became known as "The George Keats Collection." Other than my own revelations mentioned here, the original housing for the collection was simply disclosed as an inheritance; I have delayed publishing the story of its reclamation until such time as the Keats burial site was named to the official historical register and so was not in danger of being invaded.

As to what George secreted away, other than the money itself, which was divided among the inheritors, I have decided to provide a partial list so as to shed light on the curious mind of George Keats. His collection reveals not only his foresight (note the Audubon paintings, which, outside of The New York Historical Society, were found nowhere else prior to this discovery), but also his idiosyncratic interests (note the contents of the only three private libraries in Louisville). In all, two hundred thirty three distinct artifacts, other than money, were recovered. What appears below is a mere fraction of what is presently housed at The Kentucky Historical Society and is only meant to whet the reader's interest.

Partial List of The George Keats Collection

1) Silver Cup engraved with the names of winning horses at the 1839 Spring Race meet at Oakland Race Track.
2) An original, hand-written menu from Galt House listing: Saddle of Mutton with currant jelly; Red-Headed duck, stuffed; Wood-Duck with Hunter's Sauce; Wild Goose with Potwine Sauce; Bridge of Buffalo Tongue a la Godar; Arcade of Pheasants with Green Peas; Boar's Head; Fish, hot breads, salads etc. for the price of fifty cents.

(authenticated by same menu as published in *The Texture of Urban Life; Some Cultural Institutions of Louisville in the 1830s* by Carl E. Kramer, 1975).

3) Drawings for quilting patterns with hand-added notes "given by Mrs. Reynolds to me for 'poor and orphans'" (presumably church sewing circle for donated quilts).

4) Five pearl-beaded sachet casings with faceted rubies on the drawstrings.

5) Two articles (likely circa 1820s) from unknown papers: one decrying the fouling of public wells and the other calling for the outlawing of "rampantly running pigs in our streets and byways."

6) Hand-sewn board portfolio of written work titled *The Poems of Isabelle Keats* (including twenty hand-written poems, presumably by the author).

7) Seven issues of the *Louisville Literary Newsletter*, from years beginning with its first publication in 1838, and including material from Washington Irving and Henry W. Longfellow, published by George Denison Prentice.

8) A silver broach signed by the jeweler William Kendrick.

9) The contents of three private libraries of Mr. Keats, Mr. Cosby, and Mr. Short, all of Louisville, Kentucky.

10) Two children's dolls with painted porcelain face, hands, and feet; one dressed in calico, one dressed in pink cotton with a cream-colored pinafore and matching bonnet.

11) Seventeen original paintings signed by John J. Audubon (with note on the backs of five: "To my friend George Keats" written in graphite); of these, three are of birds now extinct in the U.S.

12) Nine original engravings by John J. Audubon of birds (from their "sketches" also found rolled together) of heretofore unknown works by the artist.

13) A revolver of unknown make and origin.

14) 1831 copy of original charter in that year of the Louisville Lyceum, complete with hand-written note by Mann Butler to George Keats discussing the Lyceum's goals (literary "improvement," to "promote and distribute useful knowledge through written essays, oral addresses, and discussions") as well as membership dues ($10.00 for life, $1.00 per year).

15) Matched pair of vases by the Staffordshire potter, William Prost.

16) Miniature portraits in cameo settings of Isabelle Keats, Emma Keats, and Georgiana Keats.

17) 1833 editorial circled in *The Public Advertiser*, written by Shadrach Penn (publisher), lambasting the *Louisville Journal* publisher (George Denison Prentice) for slander and libel, with note in the margin in George's hand: "Must show P."

18) Child's gold bracelet with turquoise insets; filigree silver pin; sapphire hat pin; gold watch fob; fourteen carved silver buttons.

Afterword

Distinguishing between what is real and what is imaginative is often a difficult task; that is especially the case here in that I've attempted to so closely weave elements of the Keatses' actual lives with those of my own creating. Many aspects of this novel are drawn from research, and I would like to acknowledge the fastidious documentation by the Kentucky Historical Society as well as the Filson Historical Library in collecting and maintaining first-hand accounts of the life and times of George Keats. I would also, for the record, like to attempt a separation of what is "real" and what is derived (sometimes out of whole cloth) from my imagination.

The excerpts from letters by John Keats have been embellished upon; the originals can be found in collections of his published letters, excepting the one having to do with his creation of the poem "Ode on a Grecian Urn," which I wholly constructed. I have attempted to recount the historical record of the Keatses with accuracy but for the creation of a fictitious son of George Keats—Samuel—who bore the plot burden I felt I could not, in good conscience, attribute to any of George's actual children.

The Filson Historical Society library as well as the

Seelbach Hotel are accurately depicted, and accounts of their structures and history have basis in fact. There was, as well, an inhabitant of the Seelbach named Jacoby who lived there during the time period I attributed to him as well as to Brett's fictitious grandfather.

I am also indebted to the Kentucky Historical Society for the preservation of Mr. William L. Alves' recollections of life in Henderson, Kentucky, during the years that John J. Audubon and George Keats lived there. This recollection coupled with the historical information I located at the Filson Historical Society and other locations, contributed to the creation of George Keats' fictional journal and to his relationship with John J. Audubon (with whom George and Georgiana Keats lived upon first arriving in America). Though the journal, of course, does not exist, I have attempted to draw on actual occurrences in George's life in creating it.

And though the Keats family burial plots are located at Cave Hill Cemetery, there is no mausoleum for Isabelle, nor is there a treasure left by George Keats for his family. Unfortunately, he did die in bankruptcy just as the contemporaneous record reports.

I have tried to render all other aspects of life on a breeding farm, as well as in the life and times of George Keats (except as noted here) factually and realistically.

Finally, I would be remiss in not acknowledging how grateful I am to have come to know George Keats in his triumphs and tragedies. The death of his daughter Isabelle, which occurred just as I have recounted it (excepting the death date, and that the gun belonged to John Henry, not "Samuel"), his fortitude, wisdom, generosity of spirit, intelligence, and accomplishments are all evidenced in contemporaneous accounts of him. To have come to know him in this study has been a personally gratifying experience.

228